Crimson Catacombs
Lexi Gray

Thank you!

Copyright © 2023 by Lexi Gray

All rights reserved.

No part of this publication may be reproduced, distributed, or transmitted in any form or by any means, including photocopying, recording, or other electronic or mechanical methods, without the prior written permission of the publisher, except as permitted by U.S. copyright law. For permission requests, contact authorlexigray@gmail.com.

The story, all names, characters, and incidents portrayed in this production are fictitious. No identification with actual persons (living or deceased), places, buildings, and products is intended or should be inferred.

Blood Reapers MC

You have entered the Blood Reapers MC, where we do what we want and how we want. Don't bother coloring us as the hero's of your story because while we do hero shit, we aren't the hero's here. Yeah, we do the hero shit like save children from trafficking rings but it is also a way for us to have the blood we so desperately need. We are morally gray and have no qualms with slicing throats and watching the blood drain down your skin.

This series of books is my darkest series to date. There will be a lot of triggers so please be advised before entering this world. These guys aren't good unless you are an innocent child taken from your home/school. They don't have redeemable qualities and our heroines aren't going to try to change them. Quite the opposite actually, these heroines will be just as unhinged as they are, you will just have to read and see...

This series will be four books:

- Crimson Catacombs

- Viridian Vault

- Tyrian Tomb

- Malachite Maze

Each book will be a standalone with characters that carry over from each book. There will be a HEA, as close as unhinged people can be, to wrap up each story.

For a full list of triggers for each book, please check out the website: www.authorlexigray.com

Terminology

Baffle – Sound deadening material that sits inside the muffler and quiets the exhaust.

Colors – Insignia or "patches" worn by motorcycle club members on their cuts to identify their membership and location.

Cut – Motorcycle Club vest that is either a leather or jean sleeveless jacket that has the emblem of the club on the back of the jacket and a pocket area on the front of the jacket.

Jacket Picker – A club whore who only hangs out at the club to be screwed or to try and screw their way to being an ol' lady.

MC – Motorcycle Club

Ol' Lady – wife or steady, long-term girlfriend of a fully patched member. She maintains no official roles in the club, however is considered off limits and usually has the man by the balls (at least in my stories).

Patch-Holder – A fully patched member of the club.

Prospect – A potential member who is not yet patched in, basically an intern but with more bitch work.

This is a motorcycle club romance. While there are ideas and styles that may be of similarity, it's important to note that this is a work of fiction. We do **_not_** encourage people to act out scenes in this story or other works that may be associated to this story. It is not an education book, however safe practices are utilized in the making of this material.

Triggers

Ex-boyfriend cheated; parental alcohol abuse; foster care abuse (on-screen); on-screen torture with blood and gore; open-door sex; blood play/fascination; masochism and sadism; dub-con/Non-Con; primal play; Degradation; Child Trafficking (Details off page, on-screen mentions & tracking); Self-harm and suicidal ideation -brief, on-page; hints of somnophilia; vomiting. This list is not all inclusive, please visit http://authorlexigray.com/triggers

Tropes

MM/MMFMM; Motorcycle Club Romance; Dark Romance; Why Choose/Reverse Harm; Touch her and die; Equally unhinged; Serial Unalivers; HEA

Playlist

Play with Fire - Sam Tinnez (feat. Yacht Money)
Mind Games - Sickick
You Don't Own Me - SAYGRACE
Buttons - The Pussycat Dolls
Hammer to the Heart - Teddy Swims
Beg! - Vana
Slayer - Bryce Savage
Just Like You- Three Days Grace
Therefore I am - Billie Eilish
You Want a Battle?- Bullet For My Valentine
PYRO- Shinedown
A Match into Water-Pierce the Veil
Never Too Late - Three Days Grace
King for a Day- Pierce the Veil
GIRLS- The Kid LAROI
Sad Sorry After Party- UPSAHL
The Devil Wears Prada- PLVTINUM, Shaker & Vana
Disgusting!- Vana
Ocean Eyes - Billie Eilish

Blvck- Bryce Savage

Seven Nation Army - SKÁLD

Like a Drug- Bryce Savage

Animal I Have Become- Three Days Grace

Separation Feels Similar- Alisxn Gray

45 - Shinedown

Blurb

You can run, Little Pyro, but we will always catch you. Let the games begin.

REGAN

Fire has always been my favorite thing to watch. I loved to play with it, manipulate it, and just watch how it would rage. It felt exactly how I did on the inside. It was like I burned from the inside out, and there was never an escape. I have always felt as though it would engulf me one of these days, yet it wasn't until I met them that playing with it and letting it take me over wasn't as scary as I thought it was.

BLOOD REAPERS

We have been content to seek pleasure from each other, unbothered by the nights and days that dragged by. We thought nothing could rile us up...then our Little Pyro walked right into our life. She burned brightly for us. So hot that she sparked a new beginning into us, sweeping us in her scorching flames without a hint of remorse. Now, she is ours and we will ensure she can never leave. We are the only ones who can give her what she needs, even if she doesn't know it yet.

Fire and Ice

Robert Frost

Some say the world will end in fire,
Some say in ice.
From what I've tasted of desire
I hold with those who favor fire.
But if it had to perish twice,
I think I know enough of hate
To say that for destruction ice
Is also great
And would suffice.

Chapter One

Regan

EIGHT YEARS AGO

The fake smile is already plastered on my face as the last customer leaves for the night. "Thank you for shopping at Quest Books, hope to see you soon!" The young lady waves as she exits into the night, the bell jingling overhead to signal her departure. I slump against the bookcase behind me in relief. Alina called in sick today, which happens to be the third time this week, and I honestly feel like I'm drowning with bone deep exhaustion. Being around people isn't something that makes me happy, which is why I bought a bookstore and employed it. I wanted to be around books every day of my life to avoid reality, but when the one employee I count on to be here doesn't show up, it makes that vision blur into the distance.

Just as I'm about to push myself up fully, the bells above the door jingles. Glancing down at my watch, I realize it's just after eight pm. "Hi there," I start, looking around for where the person had gone. "We are actually closed right now, but we open at six tomorrow morning. We will have fresh brew waiting for you." My cheeks burn from the fake smile plastered on it, but the allusive stranger still hasn't acknowledged me nor came out of the shadows. I barely got a glimpse of them when they entered, and I haven't heard anything since. Maybe it was a fluke, just the wind or A/C kicking on.

Yeah, that's it. Just the A/C.

Definitely the A/C...

Nope.

Grabbing my bag from the hook under the counter, I don't even bother to close out the drawer. It can wait until I come back in the morning for opening duties. Taking several glances around again, there's nothing to be seen besides the clean tables, neatly stacked books, and the open sign blinking erratically. Huffing in annoyance with myself, I click off the cheap sign and head out. It's dark outside, slightly eerie like it is every other night. Only tonight, my hackles are on high alert. The hair on my neck seems to raise in awareness as I whirl around and scan the surrounding areas.

Nothing.

"Get over yourself," I scoff. The key easily enters the lock and glides into place with ease. Pushing them back into my bag, I clutch it to my side and walk quickly back to the apartment complex I rent with my boyfriend, Jensen. He and I have been together for just over a year, but it seems to be stagnant at this point. We don't do anything or go anywhere, even if I want to initiate it. He refuses to go on a hike in the beautiful mountains, and he refuses to even fuck me if I'm horny. Two extremes, I know, but that's the principle of the matter. My mind has been made up about us for a few months, I'm just too chicken shit to do anything about it. Maybe because I have no clue what the future would hold.

Rounding the corner near the forest, I pick up my pace when the feeling of being watched seems to double. Reaching into my bag, my zippo is at the very top of all the stuff inside of it, exactly where I like it. I don't try to look around as I would rather not be one of those maidens that eats shit on the ground in an effort to see their attacker. The top of the lighter flips open easily, and the spark ignites as I pass my thumb over the flint quickly. Just as my brain seems to ease, I'm halted in my tracks with the sounds of a distant grunt. I scan my surroundings thoroughly, unsure what there could be to even see with everything so dark...

There.

I squint in the distance to what looks like a roaring fire, and the lighter clutched in my hand is suddenly white knuckled. My ears don't pick up on anything else, just the fire that seems to fan the flame of the spark within me. Instinctually, I take a step forward toward the light and zip the lighter to blow a full flame. A rustle of the trees has me snapping out of my stupor, snapping the lid shut, and continuing on to the apartment with added speed. I can smell the smoke billowing from the flames behind me, my anxiety and need for more echoing in my brain. After several seconds of the blood rushing through my ears, sirens scream through the air to signal a close end to the fire.

My phone buzzes in my pocket, then stops before starting again. Groaning with annoyance, I replace my phone with my lighter in my pocket. Abigail has tried to call me via FaceTime two times, a third time sparking my phone back to life in my hand. I don't hesitate to answer when it lights up again, ready to hear her complain and tell her what a creepy night I have had, except...

"Please Jenny," a high pitched squeal shrieks out followed by a giggle. I can't see anything except her light blonde hair swishing behind her as she bounces up and down. I'm blushing, laughing at her accidental butt dial until the phone tilts just a little.

"Fuck, Abi, these perfect tits..." the groan is familiar...one that sends a punch right to the gut. "We don't have long, come all over me. Use my cock like the secret little slut you are." My mouth drops open in shock and horror. They must be rocking the bed so hard that the phone just tilts and tilts until her bare ass comes into view with Jensen's leg tattoo on full display. Like the rabbits they are, they just keep jacking into one another as anger rips through me.

I hung up quickly, shocked and horrified at what I just witnessed. There's no way that I just saw that...maybe it was a figment of my imagination? Why would Jensen cheat on me? He would never, right?

My system is too overstimulated for this shit. First, I have a fucking stalker, now this?

"Fuck everything!" I scream into the night, my fists balled so tightly my nails create moons in my palms. Deciding against chancing my fatal flaws, I sprint around the corner and fly up the stairs to the apartment. My next moves have to be played smartly, no storming in and ruining the evidence. As quietly as I can, I move to put my key in the knob, but it opens right up as I jiggle it. Cold chills sweep down my spine when the same moans and groans from the phone seem to echo off the walls of *our* apartment. The one Jensen and I share, not that he seems to care, and thankfully we didn't get the chance to add me to the lease yet.

Guess it's only his apartment again. Makes leaving all the easier if what I'm hearing is true.

Maybe he has a friend over with the same tattoo? Who the fuck am I kidding?

Scoffing at myself for pulling straws, I decide that I need to get this reveal over with once and for all. Tears begin to burn behind my eyes at what this would mean for me. Another pillar being smashed to pieces for me, uprooting me all over again.

I never grew up in a stable home, stability isn't something I knew but I do crave it. My first nine years of life were riddled with heartbreak and pain. While my dad saw the bottom of the bottle, I saw the whites of his knuckles. Mom and dad both managed to drink their lives away yet never had enough money for us to eat or pay rent. If they weren't drinking, they were using me as their personal punching bag. Shit, I guess it didn't matter if they were drinking or not, I ended up black and blue. *I* was the sinner. They told me time and time again that *I* needed to repent for their sins. *I* was the problem. We ended up living in the car for the last two years of their pathetic lives because of *me*. Or, so they say it was my fault.

They blamed me for their inability to use protection. Not like I fucking asked to be here. Even to this day, I still vividly remember when I found my parents, each with a bullet cracked in their head, right between the eyes.

They sent me inside the grocery store to get something for them, and I didn't think anything of it. The details are so blurry in the bigger picture and I had been their gofer for years, so it wasn't anything new for me to do their bidding. I remember hearing two pops, almost like someone had pulled a confetti popper, then there were people shouting. Again, I didn't think anything of it, just continued shopping for the things my parents asked for in fear of their anger. I refused to get into trouble putting my nose in other people's business, so I don't.

The cashier at the time had looked at me strangely but checked me out. He didn't say anything, but I got a weird sense of dread at that moment when more and more people swarmed outside. When I got back outside to take the bags to my parents, several people surrounded the car. Dropping the bags by the door, I slinked my way through the crowd undetected. Turns out head wounds bleed faster than other areas of the body, at least that's according to the doctor that was talking out loud and the obvious amount of blood on the ground. It should have been a lot more traumatic than it was, and maybe it will catch up to me one day. Mom's eyes were wide open and a look of shock still painted her features. She didn't see it coming, unlike dad. He seemed...resigned. As if he knew the end was coming for him. I ran away after that. My parents had warned me what would happen if someone else were to take me, and I was not about to risk it. It was funny because I managed to stay under the radar for nearly three months. My parents didn't have any form of ID on them, the rest of our family is dead or wants nothing to do with us, and their faces were too gruesome to air on TV to help identify them. So, they remained John and Jane Doe for two whole months until someone managed to get photos of them and post them to the news.

Once that happened, it felt like there were social workers swarming the school to find me. I tried to outrun them, and I did a pretty damn good job until one of the officers, Officer Ziggy, tracked me down. Once he clocked me, we paced each other for a while, but his stamina was a whole lot better than mine. No nine year old could outrun someone who was trying to record for the Olympics. Once he tackled me, I knew right then and there that my life would never be the same. Everything I knew was going to come to an end. To my nine year old self, I wasn't sure if that was a good or bad thing. I didn't know what life entailed, didn't know if there were better things in this world, but I was sure it could get a whole lot worse.

Shaking my head from the shitty thoughts of my past, I roll my shoulders back and storm into the room. Abigail sees me first and scrambles off the bed while taking the top sheet with her. It's almost comical to watch her struggle to save face, her prissy self trying to fix her hair and swipe at her mouth. Though, her mascara is smeared down her cheeks and her lipstick is smudged from lord knows what. It's probably from her sucking his dick, and let's be honest, it's not the biggest one in the city. Though, that's what happens when people think they are too big for their britches. They get caught. From what it sounded like, this has been going on a lot longer than just tonight.

"Regan!" She shrieks and giggles as if I hadn't just caught her screwing my boyfriend. To be honest, I don't know whether to scream, cry, laugh, or a combination of them all. If anything, I do feel a bit relieved.

Also, not to be self deprecating or anything, but there is a level of pretty that I can see what Jensen sees in Abi. He's not very tall at five feet ten inches, but compared to my five feet three inches, he towers over me. Abi stands close to his height and seems to look over (literally) to me whenever we are together. She's a blonde-haired, blue-eyed girl that gets what she wants. If she doesn't get it, she will take it with no remorse. I suppose this is one of those times, but then again, I'm just a plain Jane with brown hair and green eyes. There is nothing special about me when it comes to her. Honestly, I should have seen this coming miles away. The hints they were dropping, the long looks, the flirty comments...it was all there. I was choosing to ignore them subconsciously, that much is obvious.

I scoff at my own idiocy and her goddamn audacity. "Fuck off, Abigail," I sneer as I go to the shared closet to grab my suitcases. Shoving my clothes into the bags, it takes another few seconds for Jensen to finally come out of his stupor. Jumping off the bed, he starts shouting things at me and Abigail. I purposefully ignore him while I pack quickly. Not hearing what he says seems to bite me in the ass because his hands land on my shoulders, haul me to my feet, spin me around, and sends the back of his hand straight into my cheek. My ears ring from the impact as my head goes flying to the side. Spit flies from my mouth and pain bursts through my face.

I don't blink. Rearing back my fist, I slam it into his cheek and watch him crash to the ground in utter surprise. Liquid drips onto my top lip, but my level of thinking isn't all that rational. All I know is that if I don't get out of here soon, I may end up with a murder charge. Turning on my heel, I finish packing as quickly as I can while I work to extinguish the fire in my gut. My fingers twitch with a need to light their asses on fire.

Burn them to the ground.

Watch their skin melt.

See their blood boil as it pours from their bodies.

Inhaling and exhaling several times, I force myself to push on packing. If I stop moving, I will absolutely set this place up in flames. One wrong move, one wrong word, and the zippo would be the tool I use to make sure they never see the light of day again.

Clearing my throat, I stand. "I will send someone for the rest of my stuff later. If you refuse them, I will not hesitate to find you myself." The tone that comes from me is cold and void, and it's been years since I have had to step out of my own body like this. It's a feeling that quickly gives me recognition, a sense of belonging within myself that I allow to wash over me. Palming the lighter in my pocket, my shoulders square in resolution. I refuse to be a pushover like so many females that I know, and I also refuse to allow a man to walk all over me like I'm the scum under his shoe then continue to disrespect me behind my back.

"You're not going anywhere," Jensen growls as he tries to stop me again. This time, I don't wait. I rip the lighter from my pocket, popped it open and lit the hair of his chest on fire. Shrieking, Abigail jumped into action to try and fan him off. It takes everything in me to not sit and watch the fire sizzle on his chest. The scent of burning hair encapsulates my senses, threatening to seize my focus. More deep breaths ground me with my sanity, I grab the two suitcases and leave.

Chapter Two

Warden

EIGHT YEARS AGO

Mask securely in place and the cut on my back shedding light on my allegiances, I wait for the signal from my brothers in arms. It's been a slow process, one that has been the death of us. This single mission has taken us around the world, and now, we are in the fucking middle of nowhere Utah. We have busted our asses, waiting until the perfect time to strike, and now…it's time. The Mountain Range Circuit has been running for years, and every time we hit their business, we chip away at them a little more. Tonight, there is said to be a cat house waiting just behind those walls. Sadly, we won't get the goods.

Glancing over to where Viper should be, the light illuminates around his silhouette giving him the appearance of a reaper. He's known to be fast, his aim is spot on, and he doesn't take prisoners, only blood. He must sense me looking because he turns his head towards me, grabbing the bottom of his skull mask, and he lifts it up displaying shadowed lips.. He darts his tongue over them and sucks his bottom lip between his teeth. My cock twitches in my pants with desire, but now isn't the time. If it were, I would spank his ass bright red for riling me up.

Maverick, one of my best friends, raises his fist into the air. We freeze, hesitant to breathe at all. His face is buried in the binoculars as he focuses on the target around us. Shark, our president, is down below doing recon. Usually myself, Maverick, Ghost, and Viper are on the floor making moves on targets, but Shark wanted to be the first to strike. For as much as he has busted his ass to make this mission possible, we voted in agreement for him to take full lead. He also knows that if he is in danger, we will not stand down no matter the command. Seconds later, shots start echoing from around us into the open air.

It's hard to see anything except pure darkness until a bullet whizzes past my head and lights slam on. Like a fucking football field, the lights shine down on us as all hell breaks loose. Team two storms the warehouse in front of us, killing anyone in sight. Team three follows quickly behind them and begins to remove the victims quickly. Cries of agony pierce the air around us, but I wait for my cue. Several guys engage in hand to hand, their men go without much of a fight as our men kill them with ease.

As if on command, vans come screaming through the gates where our guys are practically throwing kids into the vans. They are panicking, trying to figure out what's going on, but we don't have time to explain that we are trying to get them out of this awful place. For some of them, this is all they know. We hope to return them to their families or be able to help provide them with a better future. Unfortunately, for children that are trafficked, families will have this stigma about them that turns them against their child. Trafficking is known to really fuck up a person mentally, and when it comes to those who have yet to fully develop, their cognitive abilities can diminish exponentially. We don't know how long they have been at the facility, just that we are getting them out. That being the case, it will take time for all of them to be assessed and for their families to step forward.

As a club that helps children in all aspects of being released from their captors, we also ensure they have stability. We work closely with adoption agencies and social workers to ensure the best situation for the child on a case by case basis. Unfortunately, not all kids can be adopted when they get out of this.

"Runner!" A voice shouts, and Viper takes off. Three men have managed to slip through the first two lines of defense, but we are the final. There's no fucking chance any of them will survive. Mav, Ghost, and I follow suit. One of the three is stupid enough to look back and see Viper right there. He shrieks like a little girl when Viper tackles him. The two others don't stop when their companion drops, and they don't look back when his cries turn from garbled to silence as Viper takes his machete and severs his head from the rest of his body. The sight would have a weaker man passing out. For us, we laugh as we sprint past the wreckage.

"Good luck losers," Viper cheers, and he splatters blood at us as we pass. Ghost, being the complete clean freak that he is, grimaces in annoyance at Viper for his shenanigans. Mav and I just laugh in glee for the chase. Rounding another corner, we come up on a strip of several shops. Many of them are blacked out for the night, but three of them have their lights on. If I wasn't paying attention, I wouldn't have caught one of our guys slipping inside of the small book shop. Growling, Ghost keeps trailing the third guy while Mav stops with me.

Holding up two fingers, I signal inside the bookshop. He nods, quietly understanding what I mean. He rounds the back of the shop while I stay in the front. If I'm remembering the layout of the town correctly, each of these little shops only have two exits. One in the front, one in the back. The store is smack in the middle of the stretch, so there wouldn't be any bathroom windows or any other points of exit.

The front door jingles open as the lights dim into emergency ones, and just as I'm about to strike, I realize it isn't my target. It's...a girl?

"Get over yourself," she scoffs to herself as she locks the door. It's hard to see in the pale light, but her striking features captivate me. My entire world seems to melt away, and all that is left is her. Talk about being sappy as fuck, yet there is something about her soul that reaches out to mine. When she starts walking away, there's nothing stopping me from following her. It's instinctual to make sure she is okay, yet there's a slim part of me that knows she would be able to handle herself. She digs into her bag and when she feels what she is looking for, her entire body seems to physically relax.

She pulls out a zippo one that has the design in the metal and seems to be nearly identical to mine. Pulling out my own lighter, I open the canister top and wait for her finger to pull the flint roller. It strikes over and over again.

The forest is near, and the warehouse these assholes were keeping these kids is now completely up in flames. She noticed the burning fire, her body tensing as she watches the roaring place burn to nothing. I stare at her eyes from afar as I watch the flames dance in her eyes, she is mesmerized. They say that like calls to like, I believe them now. It's like a siren song luring me to her...to my death. Another victory and another loss. There's so much hatred we harbor for those assholes...

Patting my pockets, I furrow my eyebrows when I realize her phone is vibrating. Her white-knuckle grip on the zippo loosens as she shoves it into her pocket and grabs her phone. Moaning and giggling echo from the speaker of her phone, which is then followed by white-hot rage pouring out of her. A rustling near me breaks me from the trance, and Ghost is holding the fucker by his throat in an elbow style chokehold. Ghost looks stupefied and confused as he looks back and forth between me and the girl from the shadows. His face is exactly how I feel...confused, frustrated, exhausted. I want to know her, make her mine, but there's so much going on, there's not enough time...fuck it. Mind made up, I turn to make my move...she's gone.

"Take him to the catacombs," I grunt, watching after the girl and knowing this isn't over. "We have work to do."

| BREAKING NEWS | * Daily Quote * | SPECIAL EDITION |

CHILDREN RESCUED FROM TRAFFIC RING

LOCAL BIKER GANG DISMANTLED ANOTHER TRAFFIC RING

...e Blood Vipers recently uncovered another ...ild trafficking ring and found over 100 missing ...ildren.

...e biker gang works with anonymous sources to ...t only track down these active rings but to ...mantle them piece by piece.

Sources are keeping the children's names and appearances out of the social media light until they are able to contact the families of each child.

For now the children are being treated and evaluated at the local hospital and then moved to the group home.

DAILY QUOTE * **DAILY QUOTE** * **DAILY QUOTE**

Chapter Three
Maverick

"Reapers, listen up!" Shark, our prez, calls out as he walks in. The guys and I flank him through the doors, then stand guard at the back of the room as we watch over everyone. As chief enforcers, it's our duty to ensure the peace is kept and the rules of the road are followed. Shark has been part of the MC since it was founded all those years ago, and there isn't a better person to run the show than him. "We have been having lots of individuals attempting to make gains in our club, trying to catch us off guard when we are at our lowest."

The men and women in church all uproar in outrage, and Viper bangs his fist against the hollow of the wall to get them to calm down. They grumble about their annoyances, but they follow the silent order easily.

"We will not stand for thieves taking our livelihood. There is no room for tears or grief. We are Reapers out for blood!" Shark throws a fist in the air and the commotion rises again in a riot-like way.

"Blood! Reapers!" They chant. Shark wears a feral grin as his men stand as a united front. After several minutes of hoots and hollers, Shark raises a hand and silences them once more.

"There has been another ring popping up on the radar. Clubs across the globe have been tracking them, but they went underground over a year ago. Yesterday, Globe got a tip that they may be resurfacing close." He grabs a small folder, opening it up and nodding to Globe. Globe taps away on his computer before jerking his head toward Mav who shuts off the lights. A projector lights up next to Shark.

"Three locations have been hot spots for the rings to grab their victims. This group seems to be grabbing a younger demographic and harboring them for longer before they put them out into the workforce." Globe moves different areas on the map and multicolored dots pop up all over the place. "Red dots mean ages zero to two. Purple is ages three to five. Green dots are six to fifteen. Black are ages sixteen and up." The ranges are odd, but there are more red dots than any other color.

"How do we know these kids are being pulled for this work force in specific?" One of the prospects' questions. I nod in agreement to the question.

"We don't," Shark shrugs as he motions to Globe who brings another image to the front of the screen. "This is Kastilof. He has previously been the runner for the Mountain Range Circuit when we were involved eight years ago. Now, he is a high range pimp who runs the girls himself. One of the guys in the ring has recently defected due to 'morals changing'. We currently have him in quarantine and will be looking further into what information he holds."

"Assignments are being passed out," Keres, our vice, calls out. Being the good little prospects they are, they start passing out brown folders to those on the list. One of the female prospects, Kalli, hands a folder to Ghost. Her lashes flutter and she purrs as she tells him that it's for him and the team. Ghost, being the devoid of emotion asshole that he is, completely ignores her and passes the folder to Warden. He has been the unofficial group leader of our quad since the formation, and it's been a nice relief. I may be the sergeant-at-arms, but it's nice to have him step up when I need him to. While we do our best to make sure he knows he isn't required to be our top, he doesn't rest easy until we are all taken care of. That's just who he is, and that's who he will forever be.

Warden opens the folder and scans the contents, nodding as he mentally memorizes the details within. "This seems like a fucking cake walk," he grumbles, snaps the folder shut, and passes it to Ghost. Viper and Warden slink out of the church area while Ghost and I look it over also.

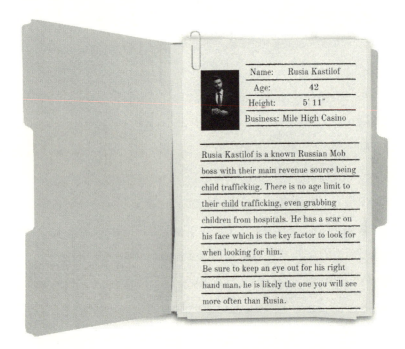

Scoffing, I slam it shut also. This isn't going to be a fucking cake walk, and I can now see that he was being sarcastic. We are the best this club has, but that doesn't mean the four of us can take this fucker down with ease. It will take a while, and for some reason, I don't think the journey to tracking him down will be all that fucking easy.

A hand lands on my shoulder, Shark stopping me from exiting with my crew. "There's a new store opening up shop above the catacombs. Might be a good idea to warn her off." Rolling my eyes, I shrug his hand off and hold my own hand out. He smirks, grabbing another file from under his armpit and slapping it onto my open palm. "Be careful, she looked…innocent." He smirks naughtily before turning around and leaving. Ghost and I wait until everyone has exited the church area before opening the file.

"Holy fuck," Ghost mutters as he studies the glossy photo. It's a side profile, not one to create distinction, but there's something familiar about the female. "That's *her*."

Furrowing my brows, I trace the hollow of her jaw in the picture, before flipping another and see her flip a zippo.

It's her.

"Holy fuck is right," I whisper as my stomach churns. She has been the object of my imagination for the last eight fucking years, so much so that I haven't been able to fuck another woman. I'm not into guys at all, but I will admit I have been tempted, just to be able to get her face out of my brain. It's seared behind my eyes when I close them. She was in my sight for ten minutes at most, yet she instantly was what I needed in my life. Obviously she has no idea who I am, but that's okay. She will know very soon, and when she realizes it, she won't have anywhere she can run.

Chapter Four

Regan

"Thank you for welcoming me to the big city," I announce with a smile. Flashes from cameras threaten to blind me but knowing I'm showcasing my new store gives me the ability to push through it. "Paperback Palace is the home to fantasy, adventure, and good coffee." Several of the people in the crowd laugh while I poise the big scissors in front of the ribbon.

"Is there anyone you want to acknowledge?" A camera woman calls as she shoves her microphone closer to me. I'm not sure if they will catch my slight grimace, but it's something I don't really care to indulge in.

"Absolutely! I want to thank me, myself, and I for the hard work and dedication I have put into making this dream a reality. I also want to thank my ex-boyfriend for cheating on me. There's no way I would have the courage to do this if it weren't for his infidelity." There's a stunned silence in the crowd, but I don't particularly care. If there's anything anyone should know about me, it's that I'm guaranteed to give the wow factor. Just as I'm about to cut the ribbon, I catch sight of something odd in the back of the crowd. Four people I can only assume are men standing with their arms crossed over their chests and skull masks over their faces. If I were an innocent little girl, I might have fainted or screamed...but the way the four of them seem to stare into my soul without getting close has my panties dripping with unfiltered need. The way their muscles bulge through the dark leather of their jackets has my pussy quivering. If I didn't know any better, I would think they were part of some gang or club.

The mere show of strength has me catapulting back in time to when my dirty fantasies were sprouting to life. How I would look at a man that screamed dangerous and beg him with my eyes to take me how he wanted me. It's also the very same impulse I have spent nearly twelve years trying to dampen away. At twenty-eight years old, many people would think I have had my chance to indulge and take what I want. Unfortunately for me, they didn't see how manipulated I was and that drowning was a better outcome at the time. Since I was sixteen, I have had this...erotic image clinging to my brain. One where I'm walking home with nothing else on my mind then snatched up and raped in the alley way. Except, it's not rape. It's them taking what they want from me, and I'm a willing participant as long as they fuck me like I'm worth less than the gum on the bottom of their shoes. In my head, I don't even have to know them. I just have to be fucked until I'm on the brink of life or death.

A throat clears, which seems to lift the dreary clouds from my mind. I haven't had a ravishment fantasy in years, but seeing those impeding men in the back of the crowd was enough for my brain to run wild.

"Thank you all again! Welcome to Paperback Palace," I call out as I finally snip the ribbon in two.

While the pieces fall to the ground, it's almost as if something more has been opened. I dare another look around the crowd only to find them gone with nothing in their wake. No one seemed to notice them, and if they did, they didn't bother to say anything or report them. Maybe it's all in my head. There's plenty of people to go around, and my first day opening the bookstore was sure to be busy. Penelope, my assistant, grabs the giant scissors from me and gives them back to whomever they came from. I don't wait around to talk to the media, instead I run into the store and get to work.

"I don't even know where to begin!" A gaggle of girls shriek in delight as they admire the huge selection of books. Think of Belle's library from *Beauty and the Beast*, tone it down just a smidge, then that's pretty much what Paperback Palace looks like. Floor to ceiling books, many of which you can locate from a ladder after you've found it in the giant book of books. It's pure magic, and it's something I have always dreamed of. For many, their dreams get washed away while working from nine to five. I didn't let that become me. Instead, I worked my ass off to get here, double majoring in literature and business, and now I'm here. Running my own bookstore and watching many young people fall in love with reading all over again. It's not even just about buying books. It's the magic in the book itself.

I also have different types of book rooms, so for those who like their romance a bit darker, they can browse in a dark academia style area. Light, fluffy romance is a mix of pinks and airy whites.

Turning on my heels, I straighten a few book stacks when a throat clears. "Excuse me?" A male huffs behind me. I jump out of my skin in fright, unexpecting company. Spinning on my heel, I stare at a solid wall of male before my eyes scale up his body to find his face.

Holy...*male.*

This man is a whole shock to the system. His dirty blond beard is long but neat, his dark brown eyes expressive without muttering another word. It's enough to have my breath taken away. At my mere short height, he's a complete tower, and I would be lying to myself and my customers if I said this man wasn't a tall glass of aged fine wine. He looks around my age, maybe a few years older at most, not that I care.

"Are you the owner?" His deep voice snaps me out of my obvious staring, and I can't help but blush.

Clearing my throat, I nod. "Yes, that's me," I squeak, more embarrassment peeking through my overheated cheeks. After another round of throat clearing, I continue. "What can I help you with?" This time, it's he who seems entranced. I'm not sure what exactly he's staring at, but his eyes seem to widen a fraction after hearing my voice. If I didn't know any better, I would guess he's having the same internal debate as me.

Whether it's the right time to climb him like a tree or not.

He must realize his mistake as I openly oggle him in return. A wicked smirk dances on the corners of his mouth as he is barely able to push it back into a frown. My brow quirks upward ever so slightly, and it's as if someone blew out the candle to stop the wax from slowly burning between us.

"Nevermind," he mumbles before turning on his heel and booking it out of here. His leather jacket is dark with a reaper at the back of it. My brows furrow in confusion, and I go to follow him so I can read the letters only to be turned by my elbow with Penelope in tow. She chatters happily about the debut opening and how well everything is going, but I can't seem to get that stranger out of my head. The mirth that danced in his deep brown eyes that almost, *almost*, shined through to me. Even in the short two minute interaction, I could see myself using his face as a seat and holding his long beard for dear life.

There's no way I'm going to sleep soundly tonight, and unfortunately, I can already tell that BOB isn't going to be much help either.

Chapter Five

Regan

Brown eyes blink down at me as I wake, my body jolting with need as his large hands coast down my bare sides. He grazes my skin like it's the hottest of fires just waiting to burn him. The wicked grin is easily spotted behind his long beard, the menacing look in his eyes seems to voice the devilish thoughts we are both thinking. His dark gaze vanishes any doubts that threaten to take over.

Looking at myself, I realize I must have shed my clothes earlier in anticipation for his arrival, but there are slight burning circles across my skin. Just as I look up, fire dances in front of my eyes. The flame burns hotly, yet it never touches me. It stays suspended in the air tipped over like it's ready to fall, the wax of the candle threatening to sear me. It's as if it's waiting for permission to bring me the pleasure I desire.

"Good Little Pyro," his deep voice echoes like a gunshot in my brain. "Focus on the flame." The tenor vibrations ricochet off the walls of my head and the needy moans I was attempting to hold in slips past my tightly sealed lips. "You're too needy for just me, don't you think?" More hands appear on my body and they hold me down for the massive male to dominate me as he pleases. I turn my head to see the *others, only to be met with skull masks. Each one of them is different, but their eyes are colored brightly for me to see. Their grip is tight and nearly bruising but that's the only way I like it. The precipice of pain is a delicate balance; a dance that I am ready to throw myself into without abandon.*

The fire twinkles brightly, glowing in the darkness that overcasts the other three men.

"Please," I whimper, jutting my chin up and turning my head to the side as a sign of submission. He grinds his already bulging cock to my entrance, nudging me open before...

"Fuuuuuck!" I groan as the alarm blares next to my head. "You've got to be fucking kidding me." Rubbing my temples to try and defeat the oncoming headache, I stare at the ceiling for several long moments while I try to calm my ragged breaths and racing heart. Shifting my hips has me feeling *exactly* what that dream has done to me. I can feel my cunt pulsing and dripping. I am so close to coming that it wouldn't take more than a few strokes of my fingers to push me over the edge. Throwing the blankets off my body, I go to scoop myself out of the bed when I look at my window. It's cracked open. I do my best to think back to last night, but I draw an immediate blank. There's no recollection in my head of opening the window. At that moment, the air conditioning kicks on.

I would never open my window with the A/C running.

One solid deep breath later, I conclude it is a simple misunderstanding between my brain and my body. I most definitely opened the window and just forgot all about it. That's the only solid explanation I can think of. Yeah, that's definitely it...another deep breath has me barely missing a panic attack.

I go to the bathroom, do my business. Turning to leave, my reflection stares right back at me in the bathroom mirror. The darkness of my eyes is new from the last time I saw myself, though I admit I can barely stand to look at my reflection anymore. It's a hollow version of who I used to be. Every now and then I can see the fire dancing behind my irises, ready to make something alight in any possible way. Each time that happens, I work twice as hard to extinguish the flame. If I let the flame open, all hell might break loose. Trust me from the personal experience that it's best for me to keep my thoughts reigned in.

Scanning further down my barely covered body, I notice a slight welt on my rib. It's about the size of two quarters placed side by side but it's almost as if something splashed on me. The tips of my fingers graze the offending splat, and the skin stings from my natural oils. Hissing, I immediately move my hand away from the raw skin. There's no fucking way...

Walking out of the bathroom, I take another peeking glance at the offending window and my heart races in my chest. I wrack my brain harder as I stand in my bathroom doorway, bringing the heel of my palms to press into the sockets of my eyes in a failed attempt at remembering something. Anything, from last night. Again, I'm drawing a complete blank. Nothing. Absolutely fucking nothing.

When I was dreaming, the candle didn't even drip on me. Maybe my dream wasn't just a dream after all...

"Nope," I scold myself, shaking my head rapidly as I keep myself from spiraling out of control. "One, two..." I count to ten as I take several calming breaths. This is irrational, and there's no amount of time that I can afford to be inconsolable.

Pressing forward, I continue with my routine. The amazing part about my space? I'm right above the store, so if there's ever anything that needs to happen, it's just a hop, skip, and jump away. I was reading a while ago that there are catacombs under the plaza that my store is in. Rumor has it that they shut down the catacombs after a massive slaughter. When I asked a local, she got teary eyed and said 'too soon'. I could not withhold my eyeroll which then resorted to an earned sneer from the girl. Further research lacked any real subsistence, yet there were talks of blood baths happening below the plaza that no one could ever truly find. People who ventured into the catacombs were said to not come out, those who wanted to prove the mystery wrong were only proven right. The alleged slaughter? People who swarmed the tunnels and ruins in an effort to stop the murders. The result? Their own death.

It's fucking creepy, don't get me wrong, but I think it's pretty fucking cool that someone thought to make these buildings have a dual purpose. It was a big deal for a few years before I moved here, but I haven't heard a peep about it since. Suddenly, I laugh. That has to be the reason my window was open. The mysterious ghosts from the unproven catacombs have come to haunt me for taking up space in their home.

I quickly jump into a pair of black slacks, put two pasties on my nipples, then throw on a white button up shirt. Reaching into the accessories drawer, I grab my black floral lace bustier corset belt and tighten it up. The girls sit prettily in the U-ring cups and the pasties keep the illusion that I'm wearing a bra. I remember hating having small boobs when I was younger. Now that I'm older and don't have back problems? Score. Looking left and right, twisting my body and awkwardly posing, I make sure the look is good. My heart thrums quickly in my chest at the idea of the burly man lighting my body up with lust and fire. Even when his eyes simply looked down my body, all my nerve endings sparked to life.

This fucking stranger needs to get out of my head. I don't know if he's the type of shadow daddy that I read about, yet he is haunting my every thought exactly like one. Shit, even two others are involved that I haven't met before. My reverse harem dreams have suddenly gone from daydreams to sleeping dreams. Not that I'm complaining. Well, I am a bit. Waking up with wet panties sucks.

With a flush of irritation, I bound down the stairs and get to work, still thinking of the four pairs of hands clawing at my body in my dreams.

Chapter Six

REGAN

Well, no shadow daddies decided to bless me with their presence today. "Thanks again for coming in, Lesley!" I beam at my newest worker, grabbing my bag from under the counter. "Don't forget-"

"Inventory, I already got it, dude. A shipment is scheduled for this afternoon, so those will get counted and added to the system tonight." Shaking my head, I know the store is in good hands. She just turned eighteen a few days ago but aspires to be an author. There's plenty of time for her to write and maintain the shop. While she's only been working with me for three days, she's already done exceptional things. She's found sellers for collectable signed copies of books that are flying off the shelves and manages to keep the media traffic flowing. She's already looking at a promotion if she keeps this forward momentum going. The store hasn't been open for very long, but I want to boast that we could potentially put the big B and N out of business if we keep going at this pace. As they say, dream big, and that's exactly what I plan to do.

Now that I'm free, I have decided to take the rest of the day to go sightseeing and just enjoy the town. It's been so long since I have had any time to myself that I just want to take a breather and relax. When I moved, it was all about getting my degrees, getting the bookstore started, and working on rebranding myself. I was twenty years old with only about one-thousand dollars to my name, and yet I managed to make my dream come true. I am in debt for sure, but that doesn't stop me from going big.

One last longing look at the bustling shop, I push my way out of the store and scan the list of things I want to do on my phone. I take off in the direction of the zoo, ready to see some cute animals to start my touristy escape.

I'm dead on my feet. There's something about running around and doing things on a whim that just has me feeling fulfilled. It's dark out, the soft glow of the street lamps illuminate the path as I walk up the city market steps, only to be stopped short when I notice an oddly placed wall. Wracking my brain, I come up short. I swear it was never here before. I flick on the flashlight on my phone and quickly realize the pattern of the brick is different as well as a slight color difference. It's not enough to notice as a passer-byer, but I have walked by this exact wall several times during the day, just never at night. Placing both of my hands on the wall, I feel it give way from the slight pressure, so I push. It shrieks on its hinges, opens eerily slow, and the sound bounces off the narrow hallway. I listen for any sounds of movement, but I'm met with more silence.

A pit in my stomach begs me to turn around and walk away. The devil on my shoulder stands taller, more fragrant, demanding that I walk until I find something. I have no idea what I'm looking for, yet it doesn't stop me from taking several more tentative steps inside and watching as the hallway opens up a bit more. Arches in the brick display beauty while there's a more...haunted feeling to the walkway.

My sneakers move quietly on the cobblestone floor, my breaths shallow in an effort to keep from outing myself. The air feels damp and oppressing, as if its hands are pushing down on you as you breathe it in. The only light refracting off the stone walls is from my cell phone. An inky blackness ahead is ominous and so thick that there is no seeing beyond it. There's a breeze in the hallway, and it's definitely not something I would have anticipated. Where could this breeze be coming from if we are underground? If we are underground, there shouldn't be a breeze at all...

Walking for several minutes, light slowly breeches my vision and I finally seem to get somewhere as I stumble to a stop at a Y section. There's two pathways that I'm forced to choose between, and I honestly don't know which one to go to. Each path is illuminated by what looks like oil lamps that paint the walls in faint light. There's not enough light between lamps to see a clear path down each one.

An audible swallow leaves me as I make the decision to turn around. I scramble back the way I came, rushing back to the safety of the outside. The stone sitting in my stomach has my anxiety crashing through the roof, and I want nothing more than to remove it by removing myself.

Turning on my heel, I'm about to go back up the stairs when a gentle but familiar smell hits my nose.

Fire.

That's all it takes for me to make up my mind and choose the right tunnel. My anxiety vanishes as I creep closer to the hypnotizing smell. Something about it isn't quite right though. A pungent and iron tang smothers the beautiful smoke.

A masculine blood curdling shriek rings out, gliding down the tunnel in a beautiful yet terrifying song of fear. It's a sound I know all too familiarly, a melody that's built purely on horror and morbid pain.

"Stop!" The male shouts and even I can admit that it sounds slightly pathetic. I take off down the hallway while he screams, his voice the perfect cover for my loud running. "Help me! Someone help me!" I feel intoxicated by the sounds, transfixed on the way the smokey smell tinged with blood guides me toward the horror that I know awaits me.

"There's no one here to save you." The baritone voice sends a shiver down my spine, forcing me to stop and plaster myself against the wall. I tremble at the elicit feeling of his voice washing over me, the deep base going straight to my clit. I know that voice, I have heard it previously, but when? Where did I hear it? I'm sure I'm not hallucinating. "You want to be helped, yet you take advantage of children who cannot fight for themselves. You get off on knowing they can't fight back...how they can't tell you no when you have them at your mercy and doing your bidding. I can't even say the disgusting things you make them do, but here's this.. You don't deserve to be helped. You deserve to rot on this pyre and wait for the devil to take your soul. Best part? I'm the devil, and I'm here for my prize."

"You're a sick fucking monster! They fucking deserve the shit coming to them!" The guy cries out, his boo-hoos meek and unworthy. Even I can tell that something is off...who deserves what?

What the actual fuck am I doing? There isn't anything that I can do. I mean, I'm one-hundred and forty pounds wet and have zero fighting skills. I'm more likely to get myself hurt than stop any of this from happening. I can sneak back the way I came, surely. They seem far too preoccupied with him to notice me.

A scuffing sound hits my ears as I try to mold into the wall. I try to keep my breathing as quiet as I can as I listen to what is happening around the corner. It's an impossible task as everything in my brain and body is screaming at me and pleading for me to find the source of burning, but I do my best to stay out of sight. The internal fight roars on, but so does the fire around the corner. It's a never ending fight, one that I don't think I'm going to win.

"No!" He shouts again and a metal rattling mixed with hitting the brick wall makes my stomach lurch. Whoever that man is, he's chained to the wall. "You don't get to fucking know the shit we go through everyday! Every waking moment we have to track our newest girl...fuck you!" His anger is drowned out by the sound of a saw starting up. My heart rate spikes, am I about to listen to this man die? It's far too loud, and I have to cover my ears from the sound of it grinding on metal. Sparks off the metal grinding fly toward the opening that my eyes are plastered to, but it ends as quickly as it starts. The sound of metal dropping to the stone has me removing my hands. My hands are shaking as I lower them back down to my sides, my breaths are coming out in short pants and my heart is attempting to break out of its cage.

"Try talking now, asshole," the baritone male teases followed by a wet plop. I take that moment to peek around the corner.

The guy that I assume was begging for his life is up on a pyre, his feet burned as fire licks at them while his arms are positioned above his head with chains. His mouth pours blood by the bucket full, his eyes rolled into his head with dramatics. Three men stand with their backs to me, all fully covered in a cut off jacket with a grim reaper on the back. *Don't I know that from somewhere?* "Blood reapers..." I whisper to myself and watch them in awe, their muscles tense and protrude from the cut-outs in the arms. Even from the back, they all look so different, yet there is one that seems to be the most recognizable of them all.

One male has no revealing tattoos and stands tall in the middle of the group, his aura throwing dangerous daggers to anyone willing to come within feet of him. His hair is blond-ish, though there's red hues in it from the fire cascading around him in flickering waves. His laugh is damning, and he steps forward onto something that squishes beneath his boot. From the blood gushing out of the guy's mouth, it doesn't take a rocket scientist to deduce what he may have stepped on. Looking at the other two men, they have marks on the back of their arms, both of them covered in tattoos and hair. It's contradicting the first guy who doesn't have any, but the difference is striking in a beautiful sort of way. They stand with their shoulders rolled back, bodies tense and oozing masculine rage. The man to the right of the blond one has short dark hair, the red haze of the fire burning for my comfort and showing just how short the cut is. It's not quite buzzed, but his long neck cracks as he rolls his head around. They all stand shoulder to shoulder, nearly the same in height as they are width. A guy to the left of the blond is also a blond, but his looks bleached and yellowing, though it is down to the root. It's not bald, yet not to the length of his friend on the other side. Amusement tickles an internal part of me as I assess these dangerous men. They could eat me for dinner and I would probably enjoy it.

More fire blazes brightly, and my internal war is waging roughly. A mixture of horror and arousal catches my senses off balance, and I have to slam my hand over my mouth to keep from either moaning or screaming. Pressing against the wall again, my head feels light and dizzy from the different needs. Seeing fire has me fighting myself to go play with it, witnessing them getting their hands bloody, and the smell of smokey flesh burning has everything in me screaming question after question.

It really should bother me a hell of a lot more to see what's around the corner, but instead I can feel my cunt gushing at the sight of the flames. I don't know what the fuck is wrong with me and yet my brain brings images of me up on that pyre while those three muscled gods have their devilish ways with me. I can practically feel the flames taking over my body as the bearded man fucks me from behind. Another is higher up on a ladder and forcing me to swallow his thick cock. The third man, the one with the most tattoos, eats my pussy and massages his friends balls as he takes me. It's not hard to imagine him and his buddies taking my pussy at the same time.

Shaking my head from the twisted fantasy, I peer back around the corner to see the man's legs nearly fully engulfed by flames. There's no ventilation system that I can see but no smoke is visible either. Instead of focusing on the logistics, I keep my eyes trained on the dying man. My faith in humanity has never been good, and while I don't think this is the right way to kill a man who hurt someone else, I'm not going to condemn them. Just as I have made my mind up to leave, the dying man's eyes roll toward me and lock. He garbles loudly as more blood streaks down his naked chest, thrashing in the chains with abandon. I know I have been caught by him, and if I don't get out of here quickly, I will be caught by the other three also. Spinning on my heel, I take off up the hallway and back to where I came from.

"Fuck!" His baritone voice shouts loudly as several sets of feet come after me. I'm not fast enough to beat them, and I can guarantee that they know these parts better than I do. Thinking on my feet, I take a sharp left and perch between a set of brick walls.

There's hardly any space for me to hide and it's nearly impossible to breathe, yet it keeps me out of their line of fire. Thankfully, my plan seems to work as their feet clobber to the ground as they run right past my hiding spot. It dawns on me that there's also the potential of them having security footage with my face plastered all over it. I'm literally stuck between a rock and a hard place. Either I out myself to them right now or I wait until they find me at my shitty game of hide and seek. There's no winning this for myself. I'm too deep to play the short game, so while they shout from across the room and look for me, I hold my breath and breathe as softly as I can.

I'm not sure how long I have been hiding by the time they give up. Maybe their tactic is that I will come out when they have their guard down? Being in foster care teaches you the basic life skills. Fight or flight. It teaches you to assess the issue then determine your best course of action. If you know you can win the fight, you suck up your ovaries and fight it out. If you're certain that your life would end in a miserable death, you flee and or hide. There is probably an in between somewhere, yet I manage to only focus on the important piece. I will hide here until I know for a fact that I won't get caught. If I get caught, I will fight to the death. Squeezing my eyes tightly shut, I do my best to remember the teachings of the last foster home I was in before I went to the shelter for troubled youth.

I roll my eyes thinking that they ever considered me 'troubled'. All I did was start a fire in the kitchen to roast a marshmallow when

I was thirteen. I mean, I may have let the flame take over the entire stove, but who is taking count, anyway? It was only me and my foster brother home at the time, and when the firefighters arrived, I remember still staring at the licking flames as they started to eat away at the cabinets. It was magnificent, truly. They didn't think so, but I admired the flames like a work of art. I remember him telling the social worker that I was a burden on society and not even the most diligent could repossess my soul. Well, he can kiss my ass because the only amount of damage I have done as an adult thus far is getting myself trapped in a lair of murderers. And even I can admit that it probably isn't as bad as it seems.

Shit, maybe I truly am sick in the head.

Fuck, I guess if they are practically calling him a rapist, who am I to judge?

Well, the law is a good start.

"Fuck off," I hiss to myself, immediately regretting it. All three sets of shoes stop their movements and listen. Honestly, for how smart they seem to be, their level of stealth and tracking is astronomically comical. You know what? Fuck it.

With the biggest bullshit self confidence I can muster, I stand from my spot. "You all really suck at tracking people," I huff, standing from my stop. One of the guys is holding a flame thrower and it takes everything inside of my body not to cream at the sight. He's tall with a buzz cut and clean face, covered in tattoos while standing bare chested for my eyes to greedily take in.

"Who the fuck are you?" Flame guys barks as his bearded friend says "aren't you the owner of that store?" Beardy scoffs in realization when I shrug, nudging his companion to put the thrower down. I huff in irritation but know better than to take any sudden movements. Preferably, the flames look better when thrown away from me, not at me.

More fake bravado to the rescue. "Yeah, I am. Also, I'm a little peeved that you ended our conversation so abruptly."

"Is this bitch serious?" Blondie says from the other side. "We should have taken her out like Shark said to." I didn't notice him at all, but his beauty is stark compared to the other two lined up with him. His is subtle, less in-your-face. He's not ugly, but he isn't the conventional handsome type. I remember distinctly seeing four men in total, but that doesn't stop me from getting my fill.

He's mine.

They are all mine.

Wait. Take me out?

Chapter Seven

Maverick

I have no fucking clue what she's doing here, but there's one thing I know for sure. She can't leave without being tied to us somehow. If she takes off, she's a witness. The only other option is to kill her, but with her scorching green eyes glancing over Ghost and Viper, I spot a sense of lust that I wish was aimed at me. Being able to note that lust, the latter suggestion is out the window. Sadly, Warden can't be here to join us in devouring this little girl...more for us, though.

As the resident re-born virgin, my three idiot friends have been working to get me laid. It just wasn't in the cards for me. I was absolutely committed to being a virgin until death because there wasn't a man or a woman that caught my attention. That was until I saw *her* standing in the store above the place we call home. I was supposed to scare her off like I have the past three owners, but I just could not do it. When our eyes locked, there was a raging inferno inside her, one that I found in myself all those years ago. She held herself without a mimic of fear, and I knew right then and there that she would be ours. She didn't have to know it. Ghost, Viper, and Warden didn't know of my indiscretions either, yet I doubt they would blame me for them. None of them have to know of my thought process but they don't really need to. This girl is going to be ours whether she wants to be or not.

Happiness has never been something I relish in. Once a person becomes happy and loved, it seems to get ripped away without a backward glance.

"Is this bitch serious?" Viper spits out, sneering in her direction as Ghost opens the chamber just a bit more to expel fire. It burns hotter and brighter, yet the girl doesn't flinch. If anything, the extended flame draws her attention like a moth to fire. It's interesting, to say the least.

"Enough!" I bark and cast my arm outward. Both men's eyes can be felt on my face, obvious shock in the way they stand silently next to me. Ghost closes the hatch on his thrower and shoves it behind him. Viper narrows his eyes threateningly on the girl. "What are you doing down here?" My voice is surprisingly soft, but her and I can both see my underlying reasoning ready to burst at the seams.

"I noticed the brick pattern wasn't right, so I pushed it and here I am." Her arms wing out next to her as she casually shrugs. "I didn't realize there was a party I wasn't invited to until it was too late." She pauses and points to Ghost. "Cool flamethrower, by the way. I have always wanted one." Ghost looks slightly shocked while Viper huffs a laugh next to me.

"Well, well, well," Viper *tsks*, slowly approaching her like she's the lamb for slaughter. He doesn't want to scare her off before he can catch her, but his eyes lust for the chase. "What are we going to do with you?" His voice drops another octave as it reverberates off the shallow stones around us. My eyes don't leave her face, and I watch as she visibly pales a few shades. She's got a flavorful tan, one that I wouldn't have guessed for being in Indiana, but her record shows Texas before.

"You're going to let me leave?" She asks softly, and there's no doubt her voice would have cracked if she were any louder. "I will be on my merry way and hope that we never cross paths again." Taking a single step from her hiding spot, Viper immediately rushes her, his hand wrapping around her throat. Her sharp inhale of breath has me holding my own in anticipation. I don't interrupt his game as I have a good idea I know exactly where he's going with this. Stepping to the side just a bit to get a better view, I watch him trail his nose along her throat, the air in her lungs gasping without struggle as he breathes her in. She flutters her eyes closed in silent euphoria even though he hasn't even done anything yet. My groan of pleasure from watching those two interact has her eyes snapping open and pinning me in place. There's a deadly sentiment that lusts her gaze, one that I don't know whether to be cautious or jump into the deep end of.

Ghost finally makes his presence known when he hands me his thrower and sidles up to her other side. Viper and him look at one another, lean over her face and smack their mouths together. If the scene wasn't so fucking hot, I would roll my eyes. This definitely isn't the time for this, but I'm not going to complain. A throaty moan escapes her, and it doesn't take a genius to know that she will be the glue to this shitty puzzle. We are all parts of a broken piece...there may be a chance that she puts up back together.

"You're not going anywhere," Ghost whispers across her cheek as he moves to her ear. With a nibble, he backs away from the girl with a clear outline of his raging hard on. "Now, what are we going to do with you?"

"I believe Regan would love to be included, wouldn't you agree?" I pause and watch her reaction. The cogs in her brain are misfiring with Viper's grip still tightly pressing against her throat and her back scraping on the bricks. "That is your name, isn't it?" She nods pathetically, one that I would laugh at the weakness of if she wasn't everything I had envisioned and more.

"Yes, it is," she rasps, her hands finally joining the party to grab Viper's wrist. "You would do well to let me go now."

"Why would-"

"Heeee!" The idiot from down the hall shrieks. Sighing irritatedly, I pinch the bridge of my nose.

"Oh," I pause, a wicked grin casting toward the girl. "I know exactly how you are going to earn your way and keep your lips zipped." Her brow quirks but doesn't audibly quiz me. Instead, I nod toward Viper and he lets the girl go.

"You would do well to stay close," I say, throwing some of her words back at her. She sneers at me but follows behind anyway. It definitely doesn't help that Ghost is trailing behind us with his flamethrower in her direction. One wrong move and the poor girl would be ashen. I would have to kill him for hurting her if that happened, so that just won't do.

We round the corner and come into view of Joshua, the idiot who decided it was okay to rape a girl because her skirt was too short. I don't know if she heard any of it, but I can guarantee that he's going to be the first kill Regan will ever have. At least, that we know of. Living with us will be the reason we bring her to the dark side. Though, the dark lust in her gaze when Ghost roared the thrower and Viper sang his bloody praises in her ear, I don't believe she's been too far from the dark ledge to begin with.

He must see her again too because his eyes light up and he struggles against the chains. She doesn't even take a step to rescue him, instead lowering her eyes to see the simmering fire and watching the licking flames dance in the coals. She must love fire, because she doesn't look up at him as he makes noises to try and get her attention. Instead, her eyes zero in on the fact that the skin of his feet is melting rapidly, the bone protruding from where the skin should be. He wails and pleads for her to try to be humane with him, but I have an inkling this female is a lot more complicated than I imagined.

Maybe she isn't all that different from us, after all. Only time will tell, and right now, I can guarantee we will have her for a lot of it.

"Joshua decided it was a good idea to take advantage of a vulnerable population and exploit them for his own gain. He thought he was doing everyone a favor by taking one for his little team, now he is going to regret ever setting foot in our city. There's only so much hiding one can do before their world tips over and kerosene is poured to start the flame." Her gaze suddenly snaps to mine, fury and something else hidden in the green depths. The fire brings another horrific element to the forefront, one that I cannot pinpoint exactly, but I know I have seen it before. The hopeless male whimpers endlessly while Regan eyes the fire again. It's before long that her face goes red with anger.

"Shut up!" She shrieks, stunning everyone, including Joshua who has tears rolling down his face. Taking several threatening steps forward, she grabs the gasoline, and pours it over the flames. No one says anything, does anything, while she silently engulfs him in burning flames. The harsh smell of sizzling flesh takes over my nostrils, but I'm more focused on the enraged female that eyes the fire with temptation and lust. Blood oozes from Joshua and splatters around as his flesh burns away, though the mess is minimal, his shrieks of pain and horror take over the room. Her fingers dance toward the inferno, but Viper slinks forward before she can, holding her wrist to stop her from making contact.

As if realizing what she's done, she takes in the faces of the room and takes several steps back. I don't know what she sees in the other two, but she takes off through the other hallway. None of us go to stop her. All of us have one thing on our mind.

Who is that girl and why do I think we are in for a long fucking ride?

Chapter Eight

Viper

The young woman stunned me into silence almost immediately. My only semblance of control was replaced with lust which is what caused me to swoop in. Ghost must have noticed the edges of my consciousness rolling their way out because he came to my rescue. Now, we stand and stare at where she decided to run off to. She's only pushing herself further into our home, and I would be lying to myself if I didn't like that idea quite a bit.

Touching her was like touching a live wire. The moment I made contact with her tiny wrist, it was like my soul entwined with hers. The brief contact we made, our eyes clashing for dominance was enough for us to be enraptured. My care and control has never been long-lasting, and the tiny thread of patience I have for this fucker and his clan is mere moments away from snapping.

Joshua remains trapped to the pyre, morbidly and pathetically thrashing on his chains as his execution comes to an end. Smells of burning flesh burn our nostrils, a welcoming smell to be sure, but it's shitty to think that she ran off at the sight. Though, I can near guarantee that *this* isn't the reason for her sudden change of heart. One tortured look at us and she sees herself in our eyes. Sees the returning look of pain and torment sizzling under the surface in our beings.

Inhaling deeply, I have the urge to turn on my heel and storm toward the main door. My home feels infiltrated by an outsider. It also feels like the beginning of a new mark, one that I'm not quite sure is the touch of home I wish for. Ghost clears his throat next to me, snapping me out of my reverie. Swallowing thickly, I tilt my head side to side to crack the joints. They rattle with a satisfying click and it's enough to get me putting one foot in front of the other.

"Are you boys up for the chase?" I ask, eyeing the spot where she took off. The predator inside of me is yearning to run, free from the constraints that society forces upon us. We are judged for what we do, yet we are the ones taking the real predator's off the streets. We don't know this female intimately, but the leash holding back my demon is fraying quickly.

"As in..." Maverick trails off, obvious concern thick in his voice. The last time I let my demons run free, it didn't work out too hot for the female. I may have gone a bit too far with the blood play...so far that she drowned in her own blood. To each their own, I suppose.

"Yes. I want to play." The demand in my own tone is clear, one that rages to be freed from the cages and chains. It's ironic since just to my left is a man that is exactly that. Chained and caged until death parts his soul from his physical form.

"Shall we make a bet?" Ghost pipes up as his knuckles crack with excitement. "First one to get the girl gets to mark her first."

"Mark her how?" My demons start thinking of ways to make this girl balance between the lusts of pleasure and the sin of pain. The ways my cock and my knife will push her toward the edge while tearing her into a new being.

A small, bitter part of me hates the idea of hurting her. Hates getting off on knowing that this could end in her demise. It's quite easy to shut that part of me away. One imaginary lock and key with the key being tossed out of my ear, and we are golden.

"Winner chooses," he quips back, his brow tilted upward in clear challenge.

"I will ensure neither of you kill her," Maverick huffs with exasperation. Ghost and I both turn to eye our brother. He may not be blood, but we have been together since we were seventeen. I know this man like the back of my hand (not the front because that's far too intimate for either of us). He's usually all for the mutilation, gets off on the idea of bringing someone to the edge of their life. He must realize that his words are odd because he simply rolls his eyes in irritation. "Do I have to admit that I'm feeling some sort of way toward the poor girl for either of you to let up?"

"I have an even better idea," Ghost calls over to me, his grin going from playful to wicked. "I think Mav should have the first taste of her. Love at first sight and all that."

"I'm not touching that comment with a ten foot fucking pole," Maverick grumbles. After a moment, his own teeth shine in the dulling fire. Joshua appears to have faded out. Sadly, we didn't get to watch as he did, but that's alright.

Our Little Pyro is ready to scorch us, and she doesn't even know it yet.

Chapter Nine

Regan

I swear to God, I can't be that stupid. Embarrassment and utter humiliation take over my way of thinking. They are fucking murderers, yet my panties are soaked from watching the fire ripple around the male's crucified flesh, and the display of their naked bodies covered in blood. My pulse quickens in horrific desire at the thought of using that stranger's blood for lubricant. They could fuck me any way they wanted while we slip and slide in the red liquid. Angry tears threaten to spill down my face as I run through the tunnels. The further I get, the dimmer the lighting gets. I don't know these passages the same way I'm sure those three men do, but I hold out on those thoughts for now. If I start digging my hole now there's an even less likely chance that I will get away.

I run up on another intersection and swing left. The floor is suddenly wet as I splash with each foot fall, the noise unbearably loud against the quietness of the passage ways. If they didn't know which way I went, they do now. Refusing to stop and listen for them, I trudge on. Several more feet and the light dims until there's nothing but complete darkness. My sound and feel will guide me where I need to go or until my sight is restored with light.

More twists and turns take me deeper and deeper, and there's a pit in the base of my stomach that warns me I'm getting too far into the lion's den. When I spot a flickering light in the distance, that seems to be the confirming factor to my thoughts. There's no hesitation, no time to turn around. Maybe the light will guide me back to my own house. A deprecating cackle threatens to make its way up my throat, but it doesn't. Instead, I'm hushed by the extravagant living space in front of me. You would have never guessed that I just ran through what felt like miles of tunnels.

Stopping dead in my tracks in complete surprise, I look around. Recessed lighting brightly spills into the room showcasing a nice leather couch, a fireplace with a mantle and a TV perched right over said mantle. The floors are still cobblestone, but they are painted dark brown. I almost could believe they are hardwoods if it weren't for the uneven patterns. The kitchen is open and I can see everything. In the back corner, a staircase goes upward into the unknown. There's no guessing what could be up there besides bedrooms, but I decide to take that route anyway.

"Can I help you?" A deep voice growls causing me to whip around. Another male, one that wasn't with the men earlier, strides toward me like his heels are on fire. Like the coward I am, I don't debate whether to stop and chat. Instead, I take off running up the stairs. His heavy steps follow after me, and with the clobbering falls, he's definitely taking them two at a time. "Stop!" His calls fall on deaf ears. Blood sings through my veins in adrenaline and something more...lust? I barely got a good look at him, but it was enough for me to daydream how his abs would look flexing as he pummels the attitude right out of me. How rough he would grab my throat with those veiny arms and hold me into place as he takes me against my will.

My core clenches as I sprint through the halls of what I'm now assuming is their home. Another set of stairs meets my gaze as I leave the hulking man in my wake. Quick assessment, there's no other option besides to take them up, so that's exactly what I do. There's no open brain space for me to absorb what's around me, but that's not what stops me dead in my tracks. I swear you can hear my feet squeaking as I halt.

"What are you going to do now, little pyro?" Three imposing men stand in front of me. How they got there, I have no clue, but they are blocking what seems to be my only exit point.

"Woah, woah," I nervously laugh, my hands coming up to stop them from advancing any further. Shockingly, it doesn't even make them hesitate as they take menacing steps toward me. Ever so slowly, they form a circle, blood splattered over their faces and torso's which gives the illusion that they weren't fully done with that guy when I bolted. The guys all look so different, even their air of confidence spirals differently than the other.

Buzz cut guy whips his arms out quickly. I grapple with him to get free, struggling as he pushes me to my maximum strength. With ease, he wraps both of my arms in one of his fully grown python sized arm behind my back. Chest pushed out, there's no chance I'm getting away without hurting myself further.

"Viper, tell us what you're thinking?" The other two men stare at the man holding me, and there's no disputing his name. He's fast and sharp just as his name suggests.

He hums and leans down to my ear, breathing right into the shell of it. The baby hairs on my hairline tickle my face, yet the heat that spreads from his proximity has my body noticing other things. "I don't know, she obviously has a kink for watching...don't you agree?" There's a slight twang in his voice, one that I wouldn't have guessed to be there just by looking at him. Instead of being disgusted like I would assume a normal woman would, my pussy pulses with imminent need. I don't know if he can read minds or if I gave myself away, yet his grip tightens just a bit more.

I can't help myself as I shove my hips backward into his pelvis. Both surprised and intrigued, my ass meets his bulging cock. His sharp inhale is my demise, and I wiggle just a bit while pressing harder against him.

"Why don't you tell us what we want to know, hmm? What exactly were you looking for? What do you think, boys?" I grunt as he tilts his hips upward, my cunt fluttering with need but not wanting to admit it. These four men are complete strangers. I shouldn't be craving their attention. *But I am.*

"I wasn't looking for anything," I hiss, throwing my shoulders forward in an attempt to break the hold. Not surprising to anyone, I don't move an inch.

"*Tsk, tsk,*" no tattoo guy tuts, taking several steps closer and brushing the stray hairs from my face. He cups my chin and tilts my head upward. He's tall, his features rugged in a way that a normal person may not find exactly attractive...thankfully I'm not everyone, and I never have been.

"Well, Maverick? What should we do with her?" Viper asks, his twang dripped in darkness. *Maverick*, my brain registers the name, and it seems to suit him perfectly. He doesn't seem like the one to bend to the will of others. Instead, Maverick leads his pack with ease, lacking the need to conform with the ways of life. There's an air of respect that swims off of the other three men that is all toward the foreboding male touching my face.

"She's been naughty, hasn't she?" He mutters, his calloused hand turning my face from left to right as if inspecting it. I want to reach out and return the touch, but I don't want to piss off the man they call Viper. "Ghost, Warden, what do you both think?" I can't tell who is who, yet I can guess because one of the men magically appears next to me. He's the stealthy one, he has to be Ghost.

"Naughty girl entered the den of sins...now she has to be punished." Ghost's grin shows all of his teeth, but it's the most unsettling smile I have ever seen. He looks like the big bad wolf, and I'm the little red girl waiting to be eaten for dinner.

The fourth male, the one I'm going to assume is Warden, sits at the back of the room with his arms crossed. He's stoic, broody, and mysterious as he leans against the wall of the hallway. The other three men are dark, sure, but something about Warden screams *death*.

"Warden, what are you thinking?" Maverick teases my nipples through the material of my shirt, tugging on the offending bud. I can't give them what they want, don't want to give in to their demands for more. It doesn't take a rocket scientist to know where this will lead, yet I refuse to give it to them willingly. *Tell that to my sopping cunt.*

"I think she doesn't deserve our time. Why waste our lives on whore pussy?" My heart stabs with shame at his words, yet it doesn't stop the feeling of need that pounds through me. After releasing a pathetic whimper from the back of my throat, he suddenly realizes that I love being talked down to. His hand reaches to adjust himself in his jeans, a dirty smirk finally pulling at his lush lips. The tattoo under his eye crinkles just slightly with the move, and I can't help but imagine how he would look from between my thighs. "Oh, you're dirty," he teases.

Kicking off the wall, Maverick and Ghost take a few steps back away from me to let Warden enter. Seeing him up close is mesmerizing. The way his abs ripple as he walks, his slow strut showcases a slight limp on his right leg. It gives him a swagger, and it makes me feral.

Slow to approach, he comes nose to nose with me as we stare one another down. Neither one of us budge, his hot breath fanning my face. My mouth salivates, and with a smirk of my own, I spit my saliva onto his face. He doesn't reel back like I anticipate. Instead, Ghost trails a hand along Warden's cheek, swiping the saliva. Ghost shoves his covered fingers into Warden's mouth, and

Warden doesn't waste any time in sucking his fingers. My mind wanders to their intimate life, and if he sucks the other's cocks the way he does Ghost's fingers.

After a few moments, Ghost removes his fingers. Fighting the grip Viper has on me, I try to shake him off. His grip doesn't budge a millimeter. Like before, he just tightens his arm even more and gives me absolutely no wiggle room.

Before I can register what's happening, my body is jerked back. I feel like I'm flying before my front is slammed against the wall with my arms pinned above my head. Pain shoots through my head as my cheek scrapes on the bricks.

"Get off of me!" I shout as I kick my leg back. I make contact with someone, though I'm not entirely sure who, and they shout before backing up.

A large hand grips my tangled hair at the roots and rips my head off the wall. "You come into our home and make demands?" Viper snarls, jerking my head to the side as my neck pops in protest. "You come into our home without permission expecting something from us? What exactly *were* you looking for, hmm? A quick fuck?"

"I didn't know anyone was down here!" I retort as I am jerked back, my breasts suddenly being grabbed and my nipples twisted. It does something to me that I can't quite comprehend. I just know that I witnessed murder, yet I'm still standing here.

"I think you're in over your head, little pyro," Ghost mutters, his voice the complete opposite of soothing. If anything, I know I'm not getting out of here unscathed. More hands grab at my stomach, butt, and boobs, kneading and pulling from four different directions.

"You're monsters!" I scream, and the second it's out of my mouth, I immediately regret it. All four men let out a menacing laugh in unison as their hands vanish. I fall to the ground in a heap, having been unprepared for Viper to let go of his crushing hold. Their bitter sounds twinge my stomach with trepidation, fear notching itself in the deepest parts of me as their large foreboding bodies trap me from running.

"We definitely are monsters, and you're our newest toy." My blood races through my veins, boiling inside of me at the heat of their gazes. I just secured my fate.

"You have three seconds to run. If we catch you, you're ours. If you manage to escape, you're free...until next time," Ghost smirks as Warden steps back to give me an opening. We all know I'm not going to escape, but at least they are giving me a fighting chance. There's a slim possibility to get out of here. I feel frozen, trapped under their critical gazes as my brain speeds through the dozens of options here. I found my way in easily enough, I should be able to get out just as easily.

"Three," Ghost starts the count. I scramble to get up, a small squeak leaving me as I dart toward the stairs to go downward and nearly lose my balance. There has to be more than a single exit in this place, that's usually how housing code is...do I really think this place is up to any fucking codes? Mentally smacking my head, I continue to sprint down the stairs and into a dimly lit hallway. My brows furrow in confusion because I swear I didn't go through any hallways on the way in. Maybe my head hitting the brick in murderous delight knocked a few of my internal screws loose. A beastly roar echoes off the walls from behind me, and I immediately know it's Ghost. It sounds painful yet daring. It's almost as if he has a feral animal caught inside of his chest, and it's begging to be released in a rage of catching his prey...me.

"Two," he shouts, I swear his voice rattles the bricks in their place. I'm making good progress as I take off through the tunnels again, but the second I'm met at a Y intersection, I'm screwed. I have never been good at making on the spot decisions, so going with my gut, I go left.

"One!" He bellows, and my panties are drenched from the thrill of the chase. For all intents and purposes, I'm fucked.

Chapter Ten

Ghost

It's thrilling to watch her scamper away, her tail tucked between her legs with a false sense of security. She doesn't realize that the four of us are deadly predators. We are fast, dangerous, and not afraid to kill for what we want.

Something in my chest squeezes with the thought of hurting her. Well, clarity is key because I want to hurt her *so good*. I want her to be able to feel every slice as a knife bares blood from her veins. Want her to scream as burning wax soaks into her soft flesh and marks her as ours. I *need* to see her tied up and begging for us to hurt her. Yet, I don't want to harm her. The thought of seeing her dead has my beast roaring as I count down to her demise. I know she doesn't realize that the moment one of us catches her, her entire life will cease to exist in the same way it had before. She won't know what life looked like before us.

"One!" I bellow loudly, watching as my three companions tear off to track her. Like thirsty bloodhounds, we split up. There's no safe place in our home. These tunnels have been overturned during our stay, and it will remain our safe place. I stand back as Warden's tattooed back disappears from sight. Swallowing thickly, I let the savage beast creep to the surface. My instincts take over as I decide to play dirty.

I spin on my heel and open a secret passage near the other side of the door, breezing down the hallway. I try to determine whether or not to meet her at the exit. Quite frankly, I think she is fast enough to beat us all there. The way she flew from the room makes me wonder if there's something more to her. Maybe...maybe she feeds off the thrill of the chase just like us...

Shaking the thought from my head, I run down the thin space quickly. An overwhelming feeling continues to attempt to break free from my chest as fire thrums through my veins. I *have* to be the one to catch her. I want to see her struggle, hear her beg me not to do it...fight against my grip as I fuck her senseless. I *need* to hear her sopping cunt splash as she pretends she doesn't want this. Want us.

As I round the corner, I glimpse wisps of her long brown hair flying past. Growling loudly and accidentally giving myself away, her surprised gasp trails behind her as she pushes herself faster. She may be fast, but I'm faster. There is no stopping me. I have my eyes trained on her as she tries to slow me down by taking turns and zags. Little does she know, she's herding herself in the right direction...wrong for her, right for us. Just as she goes to take another turn, I pounce.

She shrieks with fear, and I barely miss her as she skips to the side. I tuck and roll to a stop into the wall, hitting the brick roughly. I don't let it stop me, though.

"You're mine!" I roar and claw off the ground. Harsh breaths exit me as I watch her get further away with every second. Slamming my fist into the bricks, I take off after her again. Mere seconds have passed, yet the longer she's not in my arms, the more I want her to feel my wrath. I have an advantage of long legs, and it's easy for me to eat away the distance between us.

My hand reaches out to grasp the ends of her hair, rounding them in my fist to hold her to a stop. She screams in pain as I click the cuffs around her wrist, biting into her skin. Slamming the front of her body into the wall, I don't give her a chance to scream again as my other hand wraps around her throat in a bruising hold. In a pitiful attempt, she tries to rip me off of her. It's feeble and weak at best, but *I know* she wants this.

Freeing my hold on her hair, I reach into the front of her pants to feel her. She rasps pathetically as my thick fingers find her slit. Surprise, surprise...she's soaked.

"Oh, does our little pyro enjoy being the prey?" I groan while nipping at her ear lobe. Almost involuntarily, her hips press backward into my throbbing cock. I swear the pressure on my jeans forces all of the bars along the ridge of my dick to move. Parting her soaking lips, my middle finger finds her swollen clit, and the primal part of me throbs in unison with the heart beat in her pussy. With how wet she is, I know she's been feeding off the chase far longer than this.

Moments later, several sets of feet arrive as they heave. Looking at each of their faces with savage pride, they all wait for my next move. She's *mine* to control now.

Taking a step away from the structure, I jerk her away from the wall by her throat and bring her back to my front as we turn to face the three other men. Maverick groans with lust as he finds her perky nipples, Viper rubs his hard cock through his jeans as he eyes the meat in front of him. Warden has always been harder to read, but he looks angry. Not sure if it's because he wasn't the one to catch her or what, but I take the moment that our eyes connect to shove the girl into him. No fucking clue what's going through my own head, yet I know playing with her will wind him up exactly like he needs.

"You have no idea what you've gotten yourself into," Warden mutters softly, tucking a piece of her hair behind her ear as they stare at one another. His arm is lazily draped around her waist, though seconds later, he digs his fingers into her hair and tilts her head up. Their lips smash together, molding erotically as the rest of us watch on. Warden's hand raises, and that's the invite we need.

Viper and Maverick go ahead of us, opening the room and getting it ready. Getting her into position is far too easy as Warden and Regan kiss passionately. She's distracted and pliable as we move her into position and get her exactly where we want her. There's no forcing her to do anything right now. She's exactly where she wants to be even if she won't admit it.

"Fuck, I can't wait to have your pussy," Warden grunts against her lips as their teeth clash audibly. On instinct, I grab a fist full of his hair and jerk him away from her. I don't let him fight me as I take his lips with my own, forcing him to submit to me. He fights it tooth and nail as I own him fully. The sounds of grappling echoes off the stone walls behind us, and the small yelp of pain has me unlatching from Warden, seeing red.

Instead of attacking, I admire her aggression. She's definitely not a pacifist, that's for sure. My two other brothers struggle against her as she fights against their strongholds. Meeting my gaze as Viper finally manages to subdue her and there's no guessing what I see. Fire and lust. Smirking at her obvious failure, she growls at me as I advance. Viper and Mav work effortlessly to secure the ropes around her elbows and forearms. In the dim lights, there are faint outlines of where my fingers were holding tightly onto her soft flesh. *My* marks. I *own* her.

"Fuck you," she growls angrily. Again, I smirk at the angst rolling off of her in waves.

"Soon, little pyro," I tease as Maverick manages to rip her arms above her head. She gave two of the strongest guys a run for their money...there's a hell of a lot more to this female than what we are giving her credit for.

"No!" She screams, her fist wrapping around the rope as she yanks. She must not realize that cuffs tighten as you fight, because they bite into her wrists and form red marks, making her fingers go pale.

"Oh, you're a sight for sore eyes," Maverick coos as he brushes her nipples through her shirt. They are perky and waiting for attention, erect and practically begging to be sucked on. So, that's exactly what I do. Leaning down, I suck the material of her shirt while simultaneously biting on the rosy bud. Her cries beg for more, even as she's begging me to stop.

"Let me go," her sobs pour around us pathetically, and I know we are all thinking along the same lines. She's ours, now. There is no leaving us.

"You say you don't want this, but all of us can see otherwise." Stepping back and letting her sweetness pop out of my mouth, I grab the middle of her shirt and yank. The material rips in half easily, her beautiful breasts on display with a very thin material covering them. Her eyes dare me to mess with the black lacy material, so I grab it with one hand and jerk, drowning in her gasp of disbelief and the way the material tears so effortlessly. I smirk, then she's suddenly dropped onto her knees harshly with a loud *smack*.

Viper's vicious grin tells a story in and of itself. He knows exactly what he's doing. The way her arms are straining above her head and her lack of balance to remain upright, he must have kicked her knees forward. He's forcing our girl into submission. Just like the rest of us, we are going to *take* what we want. She can lie to herself and lie to us, but we won't stand for her to let her self-destruction get in the way of her fate.

"What are we going to do with her?" Warden asks, and while I'm not entirely sure if it's meant to be rhetorical or not, Mav answers anyway.

"Regan has been a greedy slut, if I do say so myself," he drawls with an innocent tone. "She made a bet with the devils and is now refusing to pay the price." He *tsks* like a parent scolding their child. It's dirty and degrading for her, but when I glance over at the female in question, her lips are parted ever so slightly while practically panting like a dog. Foreign feelings grip my throat at the sight of her. It's a tightness that I can't explain, heart pounding like…no. Fuck that.

"We don't ask for our reward," I say, grabbing the loop of my belt and swinging it undone. Her eyes widen comically as myself and my three brothers unsheath ourselves from our pants. "We fucking take it." We watch her struggle harder against her bindings, blood freckling from under the metal cuffs as it bites further into her thin, pale skin. I give myself a few long strokes, bumping along the roughened length full of metal, and graze the tip of my cock with my thumb to smear the drop of pre-cum. Images flash of her tied down, red and black wax burning her softness while she screams for me to stop. Only, I know she wants it. *We* know what she wants, and for us to stop at any time she asks isn't what she needs.

"You can take it and fuck yourselves!" Little does she know we like to play rough. Nodding at Mav, he grabs the back of her head and keeps her face still. I press my throbbing cock against her tightly pressed lips as she tries to prevent me from entering. Viper strikes quickly, pressing his thumbs into her jaw to force her open.

"Don't be afraid to bite..." I trail off, slamming my cock to the back of her throat. Her dark brows furrow deeply into her face as she swallows me like a pro. The way her tongue moves over the bars that pierce my cock is enough to make me nearly bust right then and there. Her eyes gloss over with wetness from the force, but she doesn't budge. A fiery debate rages in my chest when she doesn't gag. I can't decide whether to be fucking angry at her for being able to take cock without so much as flinching or to beam with pride that my female can take me like a champ. I hold myself in the back of her throat for several long seconds while her struggle begins to build again. She attempts to pull away from me, her oxygen supply running out the longer I keep myself lodged inside her throat.

Viper slinks away as I move backward, letting Regan catch her breath. Her gorgeous face is bright red from exertion, and the spit strings from my dick to her mouth, rolling down her chin as it breaks. The euphoria slowly enraptures me as I stroke her saliva over my hardened shaft. For once, I think I can agree with Warden on one thing. I can't wait to have her pussy, and I'm sure I'm not the only one.

Chapter Eleven

Warden

It's strange watching my three brothers salivate over her. With all honesty, I can admit that the icy brick in my chest thaws just slightly at the sight of her submission and willingness. She's willing enough, that is. A feeling I'm sure none of us can explain, yet we are all riding toward the same edge.

Being in the club has always had its perks, but there was never room for another. We agreed that females could be a lot to handle, and the jacket-pickers are far too clingy for our liking. Staying confined within one another was easier. Well, all except for Mav. He made it clear that he was perfectly content with his hand and fist. Now I think he's having different thoughts entirely. There's only so much we can take, and when she took us on the thrill of the chase...inhaling sharply, I replay the way her face contorted with rage. Reading it was easy. The anger she felt wasn't directed toward us, it was all an inward battle. Thankfully for her, the four of us are excellent at providing out of body experiences.

We just hope the out-of-body part remains temporary.

Viper lashes out to assist Ghost in claiming her throat. It's a sight worth paying for, and when her eyes drift toward me for a split second, there's a plea shining in them. I'm sure it isn't for help, though. No, that greedy girl wants more and there are four men willing to give it to her with no contest.

Mav reaches over to the crank on the side wall and starts pulling her up until she's forced to plant her feet on the ground. I catch exactly what he's trying to do, and with my own wicked grin, I cross my arms and watch. Her arms are suspended behind her back, her equilibrium slightly off rotation as Ghost moves to her face and pulls her down, forcing her upper body to jerk forward. Bumping Viper out of the way, I stroke my own eager cock a few times. Ghost's hardened shaft glistens with her spit. His fist bumps along the rigid barbells which in turn makes my own cock throb with glee. I have debated on getting rings or bars myself, but he damn near cried like a baby when he got them done. Her pants cover her ass in the most perfect way, yet they are in the way of what I want the most. Mav moves toward me, rotating his wrist with ease as the knife plays against the light. His own shaft is notched over the zipper of his jeans, the magic cross pierced at the end of the dark pink head that drips with arousal. I don't know how that man is a virgin. He's fucking massive.

Holding my palm up, Mav drops the glinting knife into my hand. Gripping the handle loosely, I test the weight of it by throwing it into the air and catching it. It's perfect, easy to manipulate and dangerously sharp. The best combination, I would say. Viper lurks at the edge of the room waiting for his time to strike. These men and their piercings...ribbed for her pleasure.

I move quickly, the knife dragging on the edge of her skin hard enough that blood welts to the surface. Just as her jaw drops open to scream, Viper swoops in and shoves his length down her throat. Sawing through the material of her jeans, I nick her skin each time. He matches my pace and uses his cock to keep her quiet. I'm not usually one for screamers, but I want to hear her pain. My brow raises as I finally manage to cut to the end of her cunt, several blood spots surface on her lower lips from the tip of the knife. I can't wait to use her blood as my own personal lubricant. Her asshole looks too intact for me to fuck her there, but I will put in the prep to take it. No one will take that prize from me, and she will know that she's mine.

Tilting my head to Ghost, he displays his teeth with a shit eating grin as he swaggers toward me. "Holy shit, Warden," he growls and sends a sharp smack to her ass. She jolts forward further onto Viper, her throat bulging and bobbing as she swallows him whole. "She is fucking soaked." I observe from the side as I stroke my cock. He dips a single fingertip into her wetness and pulls them away covered in her own arousal.

"I don't favor liars," Viper growls as his grip on her hair tightens.

Mav comes next to Ghost and I, groaning with lust. "Your dripping cunt tells us exactly what you want from us. Tell us again that you don't want this."

She screams around Viper's thick cock. The look on his face shows exactly how much vibration it's creating. "Shit," he curses loudly, shaking her head with her hair. "Do that again." And she does.

Without warning, Ghost shoves two fingers straight into her pussy. He doesn't give her time to adjust to the feeling as he hammers them into her. The way his fingers are curling and her knees threatening to give out, he's hitting her g-spot. She shrieks around Viper more and more, his face casted with utter bliss from her deep throating him while screaming her little head off.

"If you want to come, you need to ask," Ghost says in the nicest voice ever, far too sweet to mean it. She starts gagging as she talks around him, and Viper must be in a giving mood because he yanks out of her quickly.

"I need to come so bad," she begs loudly, her throat hoarse from the abuse. "Fuck, you're going to fucking let me come!"

Ghost rips his fingers from her and lets the liquid drip onto her lower back. He rains down bruising spanks on her ass with his other hand. My chest puffs with pride for the brotherhood all together. They work in unison to put the girl back in her place while still bringing her to the edge.

It's a fucking powertrip.

Going around toward Viper, I bump him out of the way and plug her gaping mouth with my cock.

"You will ask nicely, little pyro, or all fucking hell with rain down on your ass," I growl, sending a sharp smack to her cheek. Her eyes pop open and there's a proverbial fire burning in them.

She does her best to tell me off, her teeth grazing my cock enough to bring a slight edge of pain. I slap her again before shoving myself all the way down her throat. Her nose touches my pubic bone as Ghost lines himself up with her opening and slamming into her.

Her green irises are no longer visible, only the whites of her eyes as they roll to the back of her head. My cock vibrates as she gargles in utter gratification and enjoys the satisfying stretch. Viper kneels next to her face, his tongue hanging from his mouth as he stares directly at my cock. Reaching into my back pocket, I grab the knife and hand it to Ghost. Viper rises further up and takes the head of my cock into his mouth, forcing me to the back of his throat. My free hand weaves through his hair to keep him grounded against me.

He drags the sharp edge along her smooth, pristine skin. At first, there's a slight red welt left behind. Viper pops off my cock, gripping it at the base and directing it back toward Regan's mouth. She takes it greedily as Ghost does a second pass with his knife. This one seems to have more pressure as her blood bubbles to the surface. Surprisingly, she doesn't make a peep, but she slurps down my dick like she's scared I'm going to take it away from her, and that's enough for me to realize that she's using me as her own personal silencer. With another pass, this time deeper, her legs shake so hard that Mav and I share a slightly concerned glance. She doesn't try to rip away from the pain. Instead, it looks like she's pushing backward further onto his cock and taking the cutting like a champ.

"There will be no doubt who you belong to after this," Ghost growls as he starts the second letter on her back. The letter *R* stares back as she's forced forward onto my cock by Ghost's harsh pounding. Seconds after he lifts the knife, he passes it off to Maverick and pulls himself out. Not needing any direction, Mav takes Ghost's place and shoves the head of his dick into her. There is a look of pure lust on his face, and the resident virgin has popped his cherry. He grabs her hips with both hands, the handle of the knife smashed between his palm and her ass. With no time to waste, he pulls back and smashes into her.

Tears stream down her eyes and a sob escapes from her puffy lips around me. She gags, chokes, and gargles as we use her for our pleasure.

"Let's try this again, pretty girl." Ghost drags his fingers through the letters and presses into the cuts. She hisses but doesn't protest the pain. "If you want to come, you will ask nicely."

I release myself from her mouth to give her the chance to redeem herself. There's fury in her eyes, I can see quite clearly that she wants to tell us all to fuck off, but she knows better.

"Can I please come?" She asks, her red stricken eyes catching mine in the dull lighting. It's enough to have the oxygen leaving my lungs. Like lightning striking, there's no way we will be able to let her go. We can't keep her tonight, but she's ours for the taking and ours to do with as we damn well please.

A deep laugh catches us all off guard. Viper shakes his head with a genuine smile on his face. Well, as genuine as Viper can get.

"You're going to have to try a lot harder than that, little pyro," he laughs, his fingers trailing under her body. Mav grins as he pumps into her harder and faster, her knees shaking as Viper plays with her clit. I can hear the way her teeth grit in her mouth, hard enough to crack them.

"I want to be a good girl!" She squeals as she's pounded from behind, Mav's large palm smacks along her ass in a brutal *crack*. "Fuck! Okay, okay. I want to be a naughty fucking girl, but I will be your naughty girl." She barely has time to breath as Ghost jerks her head back and shoves his dick down her throat.

"Keep talking," Ghost growls breathily, the tip of her nose touching his pelvic bone. Mav drags the blade of the knife along her back in what would seem to be a sweet, caring gesture...

Her knees suddenly give as blood pools further onto the dip of her back. Eye's rolling to the back of her head, there's a strangled gargle before she goes completely silent. Viper's bicep flexes as he keeps the pressure off her shoulders. Ghost doesn't stop fucking her mouth, and like a man in a rut, Mav doesn't relent as he roars and fills her sweet cunt with his cum. It overflows from her as he continues to froth it into her, pumping and grinding and rutting her harshly. He finishes off the next two letters, five in total carved into her porcelain flesh.

Viper doesn't waste time yanking the knife away from Mav as he takes a step away from her ass. He moves where Viper is standing and takes over holding up the perfect girl. Face pale, she dangles loosely from the confines of her arms. Mav drags the pooled blood and drags it toward her slit. Viper fists his cock and drags the pink head over her swollen clit from behind. He looks marveled by what he sees, and as he slowly sinks into her, his eyes roll to the back of his head.

"She's like a fucking dream." His deep twang drawals from him as a growl of satisfaction slips by. Palming her sweet ass, he fingers the dips in her hips before pressing his thumbs into the cuts. That seems to zing her back to life as she grunts around Ghost's notched dick.

"I'm going to come down your goddamn throat." He picks up pace and roars. She remains suffocated on his cock as her eyes again shut from asphyxiation. When she starts to turn blue with no sign of struggle, Ghost pulls out and keeps her head tilted by her chin. Her struggling for air is a sweet sound, one that makes all four of us throbbing to start this chase all over again.

Viper doesn't waste time carving more letters into her back, marking her and signifying that she's not allowed to leave us. There's no going back for us now.

He cranks fast, his moan one of carnal sin and lust as he fills her to the brim with his own release. Finally, after what feels like forever, they look at me. As the alpha of our little gang, I learned that their pleasure comes first. Hungry? They eat. Thirsty? They drink. Tired? They sleep. There's nothing I wouldn't sacrifice for them to succeed. Surprisingly, this is no different.

"Your turn," Ghost nods toward her red tinged ass. Blood splatters drop onto the ground in thick globs, and my mind immediately goes to what it would be like to mix it with hot black candle wax. It would be a heady feeling to know we rule over such innocence...though I have the slightest feeling that she is anything but the sweet barrier she portrays.

Rounding her, I observe the markings on her back. The blood is pooled thickly and almost impossible to make out the word, yet it's easy enough for me to pick right back up where Viper ended. Her wet pussy swallows my cock easily from the abuse of the others, and I swear I hear just the headiest of moans ring out from her when I enter. Latching onto the knife, I finish the claiming of her blood, the oath settled. With a grunt, I spear the knife away from me as it savagely sinks into the wall. That's how I would describe using her right now. We are beasts in our purest form. Rage, fire, and lust. But most of all...longing.

Those feelings have no right trying to take root in my chest. Shoving them away, I tilt my hips enough to feel the sweet spot inside of her with the tip of my cock. Her head dangles from Ghost's hand as he and Mav work to keep her upright for my taking. He stares at her with longing and disbelief, a feeling I refuse to acknowledge myself. My balls tighten, my knees shake, my spine snapping straight as I come so hard, my vision goes white. She will see that she is ours, even if we have to convince her to our dying breath.

Chapter Twelve

Regan

My eyes feel like they are glued shut. Bringing my hands to my face, it's like they are made of lead. *I must have slept wrong.* The crust from the corner of my eyes comes off rough and scratchy, the bed far too soft for my liking. I don't remember it being this soft, but the way my back is burning, there's no doubt that I slept weird.

Rolling over, I crack my eyes open to look at the alarm clock. Only, there is no alarm clock. There's no window in my line of sight. Silky sheets of black are below me. Panic creeps up my throat, terror and horror creeping in as I assess where I am. Not wanting to alert anyone that I'm awake I attempt to roll over.

"Fuck," a hiss of pure agony passes through my teeth.

"You'd be better off staying put until the others get here." That previous cooped up shriek of terror? Yeah, that comes barreling out of my lungs with fervor. He doesn't flinch as I try to scramble away from him, the piercing echo of my dread reverberating off the walls and back to my ears, though he remains unmoving. His thick frame sits poised in his chair, the dark leather cupping his body like royalty. Wracking my brain, I can't remember his name for the life of me...

"For fuck's sake, what's all the screaming for?" Maverick rolls in with his hair a mess, sleep staining his face as though he just woke up. I'm glad at least one of us seems to have gotten a wake up call.

"The screaming is because I don't know where the fuck I am!" I wail, my arms spanning out dramatically. Both men don't say anything and just stare at me. More pointedly, at my exposed breasts. The stupid blanket must have fallen during my rampage. "Watch it," I growl lowly, and the guy sitting in the chair looks more amused than fearful. *He will learn eventually that my bite is just as rough as my bark.*

Maverick plasters on his panty dropping smile. I almost forget that I have no idea where I am and that my entire body feels like someone set fire to it. I like watching fires, not *being* on fire.

"You're in the catacombs, Little Pyro," he muses and strides closer to me. I rear back and try to scoot back, but my body is completely taxed. Like raking coals over, the skin on my back is taut and aflame. Hissing again, there's no way to get comfortable. Too many things are happening all at once. My heart starts racing even faster as thoughts of my inability to escape race through my head, tingling in my fingers and toes beginning as my stomach rolls. The overwhelming sensation of a panic attack is ebbing away at the edges of my vision. Garbling is the only noise I can make out as if we are all underwater.

Another male covered in tattoos, *another name I can't remember*, wanders closer to me and strokes the hair away from my face. Like tunnel vision, he's all I can focus on. His face is stoic, devoid of any emotions, yet his crystal blue eyes flow like a river through me. He looks at me like he can see my soul, grabbing onto it and telling it to let my lungs accept air. My hand is tangled in his before I know it, the friction of his skin against mine slowly waning the tingling sensations from my fingers. With our hands tightly clasped into one, he guides the pair over his chest. A steady, rhythmic beating gently pitter patters under our touch, his chest rising and falling enough that I'm involuntarily following suit.

Thumb covering my chin, he tilts my head until we are forced to make eye contact. Not like it's awful to look at him, either. He's handsome in the not-so traditional way. Taking him in, there are several small scars litter across his face and frown lines permanently etched into his muscle memory. An invisible shadow is cast over his features, almost like he didn't know it was there, but the burdens of life have forced it into place. His bright blue eyes immediately have the viewer surrendering to his destruction and power. Just like his aura, he demands respect when he walks into a room. Though, from the way his shoulders hunch and his body shrunk, he doesn't like to be the center of attention.

"*Ghost.*" It comes out in the faintest of whispers. If there were a breeze in the room, I'm sure it would have been mistaken for a whistle in the air vents. But, there is no breeze. There are no running vents. It's just him and I in this moment, and I'm not going to let him take off with it.

"Yes, my Little Pyro," he matches my softness with his own. "Focus." The gruff man talks completely opposite to his looks, and that alone grounds me back to the present. Even after his face is less blurry and the other faces are no longer zoned out, he doesn't move. No, that's not true. He gets a little bit closer than earlier. His giant thumb sweeps over my cheek as he tries to remove the running tears from my face. It's a weakness I don't wish to replay later on.

After several moments of staring at one another, someone finally clears their throat. I nod gently which is enough to have his massive frame backing away slowly. He growls darkly at the male in the chair, his eyes narrowed as if he's ready to launch himself there.

"We didn't mean to upset you," Ghost says gruffly. It sends flutters straight to my clit, and I clench in anticipation. His voice holds promise, the look in his eyes twinkle with mischief and understanding. He knows what he did to me. *Asshole.*

Again, I half-ass attempt to sit up or move or anything. I'm hit with another wave of white hot pain in my back. I can't stop the whimper from sliding up my throat as I do my best to get comfortable. Ghost and Maverick both look…sheepish? The guy in the chair doesn't say a word, doesn't blink or show any level of emotion. A fourth guy, one that I recognize as the one who slinks around in the dark, just smirks like he's proud of something.

What am I missing?

"We need to change those bandages soon," chair guy calls over to me, snapping my attention back to him. Several deep breaths later, and I finally understand what the fuck he's talking about. It takes a single glance to my side for me to see dark spots crusted in the sheet next to me. Red tinges my pale skin by my ribs while soft red drops are dried to my skin. "They are far too soiled for that to be good for her, and we don't want her to get an infection."

"I got it." Maverick strides to a door behind the other guy I can't remember the name of. Disappearing, there's shuffling and banging as he searches for something. In an instant, the unnamed guy is at my side, my chin in his hand and his plush lips slam against mine. *Viper. That's who he is.*

"That's right, darling girl," his deep drawl tickles a dark piece of my brain. It's quite unconventional, to be honest. He looks farthest from any sort of country bumpkin, yet his deep southern accent soothes an ache I didn't know I had.

"What am I doing here?" I finally ask the god-forsaken question. The three of them stare at me with incredulous eyes as if I should know why I'm laying in one of their beds. Before I can reiterate my need for answers, Maverick strides back in and motions for me to stand. My body follows his command without hesitation dragging the top sheet with me to cover my front. Another flame of fire burns along the skin on my back, but I don't let it stop me. They will see me as weak, and I won't have that.

"What happened to my back?" I attempt to gain their attention once more, but I seem to be lost on them for right now. All four of them watch me with different emotions on their faces. Well, Ghost doesn't seem to have any emotions at all, but there's still a glimmer of *something*.

"You're in for a treat," chair guy says and finally stands. He towers over me even from the other side of the room. It doesn't take long for him to eat up the distance between us and he's suddenly in my face, nose to nose with me. His hot breath fans across my face, either his teeth are freshly brushed or he has minty gum in his mouth. On its own accord, my tongue darts out to try and lick up some of the flavor in the air between us. *Warden*. Unlike the other three, the remembrance of his name doesn't spark glory. No, it sparks a deep seated fear in my stomach that has it twisting relentlessly. Just as I'm about to make a dash for the exit, my hair is grabbed, my body is spun, and my chest is smashed into the silky sheets. Anger and lust rise in my stomach, irritation flaring brighter than either one of them.

"Get off of me!" I groan, my body betraying me even more. Even I can hear the lie blaring in the room. A chorus of growls reverberate around me, and I swear the bed vibrates too.

"She obviously didn't learn her lesson last night," Maverick mutters followed by a *tsk, tsk, tsk*. Disappointment floods me, the feeling unnerving because I have no idea what I did wrong. "You are *ours*."

Also, why the fuck would I be disappointed in myself?

A pair of rough hands grab my ass cheeks, spreading them apart as I lay completely still. I will my body to move, try to push his hands off of me, *anything*. Yet, here I am, accepting his touch like a preening cat.

"I don't know, she seems to be purring like the good listener I know she is," Ghost coos menacingly. It's meant to be a taunt, I know this for a fact. Fuck all if it doesn't push all of my buttons, both the good ones and the bad ones. "What do you think, Warden?"

Who knew I had a praise kink?

"She slipped up yesterday by taking off on us, but I think she will be more than happy to make it up to us," Warden responds. More movement trails around me, and I can't see much since my face is squished into the bed

"I think our girl needs to learn a valuable lesson, what do you think?" Viper asks. Panting, I forget everything around me and focus only on the energy the four of them throw off. They are hot, heady, and ready to steam roll me into oblivion. I tilt my hips back in an attempt to get more friction, but the burning sensation is back in full force.

"She does," Ghost responds deeply, "but she also needs those wounds looked after." Like a meteor slamming into Earth, I came back from head space in full force. Wiggling seems to do me no good, moving hurts everything all together.

Tears prick the back of my eyes when the pain seems to go from a ten, to a twenty. There's only so much I can take, and they seem to be dragging this on longer and longer.

"We will get you something for the pain," Ghost growls roughly and heavy stomps grow distant.

"Don't worry, Little Pyro, we will take good care of you." I'm about to put up a fight, push them off of me and tell them to shove it where the sun don't shine...then there's a needle shoved into my neck and the words are suddenly lost on me.

Chapter Thirteen

Maverick

Seconds after the needle leaves her neck, the fighting energy drains out of her. Having her pliable beneath our hands is a heady feeling. I know she didn't pass out on her own, yet still knowing she is building trust with us is enough. I take a few steps away from her sleeping form and try to shake off the feelings that threaten to crowd my head.

She's waiting for you...

Viper catches on quickly and slinks closer. His hands grab my shoulders and pull me away from her. My brain is droning on for my need to be close to her, make sure she is taken care of and treated right. She's a fucking princess whether she admits it or not.

"Give her some space," Warden chides softly as he takes a rag and wipes away the bead of blood that pooled from where the needle poked her neck. It's fucking crazy that my conscious thinks there is something wrong with what I did. She was miserable, and I put her out of her misery. Easy.

"Let's get these cleaned up and get some of that paste shit on there before they get infected." Ghost sees the bottle of goop before I do, catching it effortlessly and handing it to me. Inhaling several deep breaths, I ground myself harshly and nod with resolution.

I may not have been the only one to put her in this predicament, but I sure as well won't be the only one to help her either. Team player and shit.

"I swear I heard some chick squealing-" Shark snaps as he slams the door open to our bedroom. We don't stay at the club house due to...proclivities with one another, but Shark has no fear barging in on us as if we were in his house. "What the fuck happened here?" He eyes the girl quietly laying face down on the bed. Pinching the bridge of his nose, he looks so fucking disappointed.

"It's not what it looks like." Finally snapping out of my surprise, I know what this must look like. "She isn't dead or anything. We got carried away and had fun with her. Our girl is a bit of a masochist." My smirk feels plastic, but Shark seems to take the bait.

"Shit, I can see that," he laughs with Ghost and Warden. Viper looks ready to pounce and gouge his eyes out. I can admit that I feel the same. "Fuck, you really claimed the bitch?"

Red.

Pouncing over her soft form, I grab Shark by the collar of his cut and slam him into the wall. Knowing that I'm not a serious threat, he just chuckles at my antics. The dick is just as blood hungry as the rest of us, psycho as all hell.

"Relax big guy, she must mean something to you crazy lot for you to stake your claim on her." Shark shoves me off of him, brushing the imaginary dust from his jacket. He eyes where we carved our oath into her back and he nods in approval. "Might have to make that an ol' lady staple."

REAPERS.

Carved in big, jagged letters on her pale skin is our oath. Our brotherhood. Our allegiance. Our ol' lady.

"You have no fucking clue," I mutter as I shake my head to clear it of the homicidal thoughts. Shark may have the balls to trot in here like he owns the fucking place, but one of these days he is going to get his fucking cock sawed off by a female. When that day comes, it will be our turn to laugh. I know she will be safe to enjoy the club. Since Shark is a known man-whore, there's a lack of trust that she will be safe from him. Safe from any of them for that matter.

Maybe we should tattoo our names on her forehead.

"We aren't fucking doing that," Warden sighs while pinching the bridge of his own nose. Oops, I must have said that outloud. "Did you need something?" He turns to face Shark who seems to sober up a bit.

"Yeah, I actually did. There has been an uptick in sightings near the location given in the folder. Three more victims have been taken." He pulls something out of his pocket and hands it to Warden. "Hotspots are marked on that flashdrive, the coordinates to each one placed behind strict firewalls by Globe. You shouldn't have a hard time gaining on them."

"Have they gotten closer?"

"Negative, but Globe was able to get some help from the Stallions of Steel MC, who assisted in the dismemberment of the defected member. The numbers and data are all on the drive, but none of it is making any sense, even to Globe and his team. Something fishy is definitely going on. I need you all to get control of it before other cartels and shit start thinking we are fucking weak." Shark looks each of us in the eyes, pressing his point home. We aren't fucking weak, that's for damn sure, and his insinuating of it has all of our male egos working overdrive. Looking over at Regan, he nods slightly. "She can't go."

I'm about to cause a fucking scene when Warden's fist flies into the air, haulting my demands.

"You're right, she can't."

"What the fuck, dude?" Ghost asks this time, sharing my distaste in the idea.

"She is a liability. Lack of training, lack of ability to ride, and lack of ability to function at the moment," he emphasizes his point by waving his open hand toward her slumped form. Her pert ass sticks in the air while the rest of her is slumped.

"What are we going to do with her?"

"You can take her home," Shark starts but is cut off by a menacing growl. Viper is not too keen on the idea, and I can't say I blame him. "Or, you can bring her to the club and we can keep her safe from there." Another growl is added to the mix. Ghost doesn't enjoy that idea either. "Third option is you kill her." Now we are all fucking angry.

"Enough," Warden demands, and our irritation floods through the atmosphere. "When do we leave?"

"Three days. You need to ensure that teams are ready to move, the princess has to have a guardian that you need to secure. Be prepared, men. This is war."

Chapter Fourteen

Regan

I have no idea what is actually wrong with me. My head pounds like I have been stomped by a thousand fucking gorillas and my pussy feels fucking spent. Clenching my ass, it's good to know the back door is still intact. I don't know if it will be for long…

Shooting upright, I scan my surroundings again. The same lush black sheets caress my overheated skin still, my back feels far too tight for my body, and my stomach pinches with the need to vomit from sitting up too fast. It's a difficult task, but I manage to swing my legs over the edge of the bed and stand upright. The furniture in the room spins for a few moments before righting itself. Maybe it was me who got a grip since I'm currently white-knuckling the end of the bedpost. Potato, tomato.

The dark walls are near barren, no scary alpha men waiting in a looming corner to jump out at me. For the first time in what feels like a few days, I breathe a sigh of relief. There's a small inkling inside of me that has to reward the men for helping me rest easy. My usual bouts of nightmares and terror were nowhere to be found. Instead, my eyes closed then opened however many hours later.

Shit. The store! Hobbling to the curtains, I rip them back and am immediately pelted with nothingness. Of course they would have fucking curtains in their dungeon area. Gives their prisoner's a sense of home just to fuck with them. Growling lowly, I pinch my body tightly just to get a few steps to the door. It creeks open on its hinges, yet I don't hear any commotion whatsoever. Taking that as my sign, I tiptoe from the room and slink down the hallway. Quite frankly, I am not known for my stealth or agility, and I definitely don't want to prematurely give myself an award, but a nice pat on the back will be presented when I get home. The corners in this place seem to be endless, but there's a vague familiarity to the way the bricks lay. It's almost as if they are telling me which way to go. I'm going fucking crazy, I know. Don't fucking judge me.

The kitchen has to be around here somewhere too. My stomach feels like it's gnawing at itself, the lining threatening to eat its own flesh.

"She needs our protection!" A male voice suddenly roars. Jumping in surprise, I smack my hands over my mouth and pray the slight *smack* didn't alert them to my presence.

"She has been without our protection for *years!* There's no targets on her and she's not been brought into the light with us," Mav scolds. It's easy to hear his voice and tell the difference from the others. In my head, the sound gives off chocolate silk vibes. It's dark, rich and smooth, and he could honestly convince me to do just about anything.

Until I remember the fucker stabbed me in the neck with a goddamn needle.

Prick.

"Shark saw her. That's as good as announced," Viper hisses, his southern twang buried deep inside his tone. From what I can tell, when he's really angry, it comes out tenfold. "There's no escaping us, you all know this. We *marked* her as ours. She's got our symbol on her back. It takes one fucking person to see that and they would know she's ours. What more could you want from her? If they even see her exiting this location, she's as good as dead."

I feel myself go pale. I didn't leave my asshole of an ex just to be scooped back into maniac valley.

Wait. Marked me?

"Those scars will fade if she keeps cream on them, it doesn't have to be permanent," Ghost scoffs like he's trying to convince himself along with the others. "We don't have the capacity for her right now. If anything, she is dead weight to us, and Shark said it himself that we don't have a babysitter for her. She is of no use to us besides a warm hole to stick our dicks into. We need to cut our losses and quit obsessing over her. The club can't take on more people until we finish our job. Once that's over, we can find another female."

Dead weight.

"You fucking cunt!" My foster father grabs a knife from the counter, shoving the tip into my nose. I whimper like a fucking useless idiot because my body never learned the other two F's of life. I freeze every damn time. "When will you start doing anything around

here? We feed you, house you, bathe you, and you have the audacity to deny us?" His screams are horrid, and as I turn to the side, my foster mother is scraping a line of blow. Her bloodshot and dilated eyes dance around us as she watches our interaction. She's been acting worse for wear lately, and when she grabbed my butt and squeezed, I ran. Foster daddy didn't like it. Fuck, what was a thirteen year old supposed to do when you fake mommy dearest was feeling you up?

"I-I-I'm sorry," I sob as my chest wretches. Vomit slowly builds inside my trachea, but I force it back down. Puking my guts out will only make him more angry.

"You aren't fucking sorry!" He screams, bringing the knife back and slamming it into the cabinet next to my head. My own scream echoes into the kitchen, and the foster mommy is giggling to herself as she gyrates on the couch, leans down, and pulls a line through the straw.

"I won't do it again," I beg. I'm shaking like the pathetic leaf that I am, my body on fire with a need to drown my sorrows. I have never thought of hurting myself, but right now, I wish the ground would swallow me up.

"You're just dead fucking weight," he growls, kneeling next to me and grabbing my face in his hands. "You have no use other than that virgin fucking pussy. You will sell it and make me some fucking money." He acts like the goddamn government doesn't pay him to take care of me. Looking over at his wife, he gives her a smile that makes my bones creak with terror. There is nothing romantic about *these two. Standing tall, he rears back his boot and slams it into my cheek.*

Game over.

Gasping, my heart is going to rip itself out of my chest with each pressing beat it drums. The voices are still yelling at one another from down the hall and my tears burn in my throat. They are right. What more is my purpose in life than to be someone's play thing? Jensen played with me all those years ago, toyed me along for his satisfaction. I hardly know these four men, yet something about them…I can't put my finger on it, but there is a helpless feeling that I can't avoid with their nasty words. I'm a burden on them. It's not like I fucking asked them to do anything for me. They chased me, not the other way around.

Though my back is on fire, I straighten it. If they don't fucking want me, then who will? The pit in my stomach grows larger and blacker with each step I take to leave. None of them seem to hear me as I slowly walk away. Moving faster would be easy if my body didn't feel as though I was run over a million times by a dump-truck. Either way, I know what I need to do.

There's no hope for me, and if what they are saying is true, I will never be able to live a normal life again. If I cut my losses now…they wouldn't give a shit. No emotion emanates from the large tattooed bully, and I know he's serious. I have no use. Weak, pathetic…

Game over.

Chapter Fifteen

Ghost

She's not fucking replaceable. Something about the small brown haired female laying in the bed upstairs has the demon inside of me fucking *purring*. There's no going back from having her with us, and that's something I don't want to even think about, yet here we are. The words spewing from my mouth are absolute bullshit. Mav stares at me like he knows everything I'm saying is all lies. Nothing good has come to us, and from the conversations we have had in the past, I refuse to put her in danger. There's nothing more I would love than to have her curl in my arms while I hide her away from the world.

Still, I scoff at their idiocy. "Those scars will fade if she keeps cream on them, it doesn't have to be permanent. We don't have the capacity for her right now. If anything, she is dead weight to us, and Shark said it himself that we don't have a babysitter for her. She is of no use to us besides a warm hole to stick our dicks into. We need to cut our losses and quit obsessing over her. The club can't take on more people until we finish our job. Once that's over, we can find another female." Bile rises in my esophagus. My cheeks burn hot with the lie, but none of them argue with me. We all know that we can't keep her. What's that stupid fucking saying? Let something go, if it's meant to be, it will come back?

"Shark gave us two days to come up with another plan," Viper mutters, his fist rubbing at his chest like it physically hurt him to be having this conversation. I think we can all relate to that, though. Grabbing Warden's hand, he gives me a reassuring squeeze.

"We can figure it out, but right now, we need to go check on her. She was knocked out cold when we left, she needs to wake up with us there. Even if we can't be with her, she will have our protection." The beast roars deeply in my chest at the thought of throwing away this girl. She was made for us, every molecule sculpted to pure perfection.

"No." Mav shakes his head harshly, his fingertips digging into his temples roughly. "No, we aren't letting her go. There's no way I'm willing to let her go. There are plenty of guys in the club that owe us favors for shit, we can definitely tell them to watch over her."

"You think that is going to bode over well?" Warden finally asks as he straightens his back. I know he's thinking exactly what I am. Our cocks talked before our brains could register what was happening. "They will think we are pussy whipped then our credibility might go right down the toilet. There's a safety in having her distanced from the club, and I think it's wise that we keep her away for now until we can figure out our own shit. No doubt she has her own life to be dealing with. She has a business, we can't take her away from that."

"Stop talking fucking sense." Viper rolls his shoulders back and grumbles. Shifting from foot to foot, he looks torn between angry and sad. "You all know that she's not just another fucking pussy," he spits the words like they are infected with poison.

"You're right, she's not. You need to think with your brain, though. Right now, she isn't safe. Think about the demographics page Shark gave us," Warden grabs the hard drive and squeezes it in his palm. "There's a bigger demographic of older individuals being trafficked. Think about the ramifications on *her* by remaining around us. It will put her in danger, and now we just put a giant target on her back. Literally."

My brain is fried with too much information. All I know is that our crazy girl is laying in bed waiting for us. Turning on my heel, I leave them to their bickering while I go look for her.

How can we be so fucking dense? We knew the potential for bringing her into our group, the looks and comments we would get for it, but none of that mattered. When I saw her the first day, I wanted to drop to my knees and worship her. I also wanted to grab my shibari and tie her up into a beautiful hanging fawn. She has the perfect shape for intricate designs and her pale skin would easily redden with the pressure of the ropes. She may not have known it was us under the masks initially, but it wasn't hard to see the recognition in her eyes when she watched *him* roll up in flames.

The fascination in her eyes while the fire raged on has my cock hardening again. She is ours, embedded in every molecule of our beings. Shaped to perfection *just for us*. I refuse to believe anything other than that.

Taking the stairs two at a time, I hustle my way through the halls. It hasn't been that long, yet being away from her for even two hours feels like an eternity. My brain is in shambles, and if I wasn't cognizant of that fact, I would actually debate leaving my brothers in arms. Since I do know that I'm slightly crazy and very possessive, I also can't bear the thought of them being with anyone else. Even Mav who doesn't participate but gladly watches. A piece of me would die if I lost any of them. Even with the shortened time I have had with Regan, it's scary to say that's exactly how I'm feeling about her too. One night was enough for my soul to infuse with hers, and that's enough for me.

The door to her room is ajar, yet I don't want to disrespect her space, so I knock. After several seconds of no answer, I knock again. No answer. Growling with irritation, I knock harder. Still nothing. "Fuck it," I grumble and shove the door open. The knob slams against the wall with force, but that's not what startles me. The bed is neatly made, throw blankets folded over the end of the bed. Panic rises in my throat as I call out for her. "Little Pyro?" Thick saliva travels down my throat in terror at the possibilities. "Little Pyro, where are you?" I shout, darting into the bathroom. Chest tightening, there's a shitty realization that hits me like a two ton truck.

She's gone.

Chapter Sixteen

Regan

Stumbling into the apartment above the store, I manage to unlock the door with shaky fingers. Rage builds in my stomach. How fucking dare they? They spew bullshit about how I'm theirs, that they own me, blah blah. Obviously they were just talking out of their ass, and I am so sick of men trying to dictate my life by 'owning' me. I have no idea how to even act at this rate. It feels as though my heart was ripped out of my chest and hand delivered to the blood reaper himself. Standing upright at this moment seems as much a chore as washing dishes or folding the laundry. All the energy that was in my body is now completely gone, and I honestly feel like giving up.

She's as good as dead.

I might as well be. What is there to live for, exactly? I have a bookstore that could be run by my assistant. I have an apartment that could be rented out to help pay the mortgage loans on the store itself. There is old, dusty furniture that could go toward the same things, sell them off and make them worth someone's while. The end of the road seems a whole lot closer than it did all those years ago. Looking back, I don't know why I didn't follow through with it...

Brown eyes. A glaring pair of brown eyes that I thought I imagined have popped up again in my real life. My dreams have slowly become a reality, and I can't tell whether my imagination is simply running away from me or not. Now...scoffing at myself, there's no going back. Those brown eyes agreed that I'm nothing more than a piece of meat to them. Warden's blue eyes also pop into my mind, like the depths of hell have been hiding under the surface, yet I could not place them...until now. "Shit," I whisper to myself in shock. I know those eyes. Eight years ago, they stared at me as I stared at them. If he saw me staring at him, he never acknowledged it. The damn call interrupted me from debating on going toward the flames or walking to him. It didn't matter anyway, because not only did the call become one of my nightmares incarnated, but it also proved that I will continue to be nothing to someone. No matter if they are new or not, no one wants me. That's all I will ever be to anyone. Nothing. No one. Dead.

The bathroom door is still open from when I left yesterday, and my toiletries are all in the same place. That puts some of my anxiety at ease. Shuffling through everything, my razor lays under the bottom pouch of my go-bag. You never know when you're going to need quick relief. Frankly, I'm surprised the men didn't notice the slew of scars covering my thighs. Then again they weren't really paying attention to that part of me.

Biting my bottom lip, I recount everything all over again and let the embarrassment take over me a little at a time. I totally let four strangers rail me into the next week...I can't show my face for at least the next lifetime. No fucking way.

Grabbing my phone, I quickly shoot off a text to Penelope, my assistant.

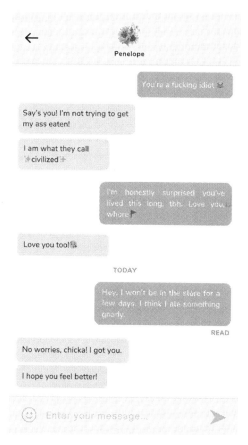

A knock on my door catches me off guard. Freezing, I listen for more movement. Moments later another series of knocks rings through the room. Like the strong woman that I am, I drop to the ground and sit in utter silence by the cabinets in the kitchen. Pain radiates through my back when I lean backward. I'm not going to be *that* person in a horror movie. Banging echoes loudly, and I swear it comes from inside my apartment. Barely able to breathe, I wait for something else to happen. Anything to make me run for the fucking hills. Several more minutes of silence later, I finally debate with myself whether to stand up and check the peephole or go lay under the covers to keep the boogeyman away like a good grown adult should. My concept of time is misrepresented by the time I decide there's no threat to my life.

Tiptoeing to see out the peephole, it doesn't take long for me to assess the lack of people on the other side. Several deep breaths are needed before my ovaries square up and let me open the door.

Nothing.

A nervous giggle echoes through the hallway as I realize I have talked myself in a circle. Someone had to have slammed a box down or something stupid, and the fact that I'm already on edge doesn't help anything. Shutting the door, something in my peripheral catches my attention. A black box sits on my doormat. Furrowing my brows, I do my best to wrack my brain on what could possibly be in this. The entrance to my apartment above the store is around the back, so there's only so many people that would even have access. My fingers itch to call one of the guys...*she is of no use to us besides a warm hole to stick our dicks into.*

An inferno burns hotly inside of me from the absolute audacity they have. Bending down, I attempt to lift the box when the bottom falls out. Red liquid spills quickly, splattering the floor and my legs. The rancid smell is one that sends me back to my childhood. That's a dead body. Quickly, I let go of the box which spills the contents everywhere.

I never believed to have a weak stomach, but when I say there was enough blood to put back in the human body draining out of this box, I mean it. Swallowing the scream rising in my throat, I stand and stare at the head that finally rolls out with the box. There, on the very top, is the head of Maverick. This time, I let the scream rip from my throat. Terror erupts from me at the thought that I was just with them not even an hour ago, yet he's *dead*. Before I can stop it, bile rises through my throat and quickly leaves me as I bend to the side to avoid getting more fluids on him. Slamming my door shut, I struggle to breathe as tears race down my face. There's no comprehending what I just saw. Those dark eyes bore into mine, the only difference is that his eyes are completely soulless.

Pushing off the door, I realize I need to tell the guys. They need to know that he's fucking dead, and I have no idea who would do that shit. Eyeing up the kitchen counter where my phone lays, I debate whether I will pass out walking over there or if I'm okay to get to the stool. I decide to brave the trek, taking three steps before arms wrap around my torso.

"No!" Fingernails digging into the attackers skin, I claw and scratch in an attempt to break free from their strong grip. Words are spat toward me as the arm releases me, and I spin, ready to light their ass on fire... "Mav?" I whisper in horror, seeing his brown eyes shining with utter confusion. The other three males are also there, muttering among themselves. I'm sure I look absolutely rabid as I flip between the four of them with a mirrored look of shock. If he's not dead, then who is? Ripping out of his grip, my heart hammers heavily as I run, flip around, open the door, and grab the head with my bare hands. They gawk at me as I stare at the dead man as his blood trails behind me. Shoving it toward them, I can't help the bubble of hysteria creeping up my throat. It's not funny, I know that, but when the giggle releases itself from my mouth, I double over in fearful laughter.

Ghost takes the head with ease, not bothering to display any type of emotion while Maverick scoops me into his arms right as my knees give out. Without him, I would be sprawled on the floor in fits of laughter and horror. I know laughing isn't the solution here, but it's fucking hilarious that the dead guy looks so much like Maverick. The three others are eyeing the head oddly, their own way of trying to connect the dots but struggling also. Their faces and confusion bring forth another howl of laughter. Viper grins darkly, matching my energy and internal rage. Who would do something like this? Who thought, "let's drop a random dude's severed head at a random chick's doorstep today".

"He really could be your doppelganger," Warden mutters when the head reaches him for inspection. The laughter subsides, but nausea quickly replaces it. Bile rises in the back of my throat when

I jerk out of Maverick's hold and take off to the bathroom. I barely make it when vomit comes rolling up my esophagus and into the toilet. Calloused fingers graze my neck as my hair gets pulled away from my line of sight.

After I finish, Maverick pulls my hair back into a simple braid and caresses my cheek softly. "Are you okay?" His deep, velvety tone encompasses me in warmth. He tucks the straggling baby hairs behind my ears as I nod up at him. "You're not going to pass out?" I shake my head, and he takes a single step backward. The space between us feels like a giant void suddenly opening up in my chest. I go to speak, but he lays a single finger over my lips. "Brush your teeth then come out to the living room, Little Pyro. We will take care of it."

Opening my mouth to protest, I quickly snap it shut when he gives me a stern glare. He turns on his heel, and I set to work on brushing my teeth. The sour taste in my mouth quickly subsides as I scrub it with mint toothpaste.

Who would want to traumatize me like that? That's not Maverick, obviously. I want to know who it is and why someone would kill a person that looks exactly like Maverick. Another question to ask is why they would place it on *my* doorstep. Without the guys, I have no idea what I would have done. One thing for sure, the cops would do nothing. I have called them in the past for things beyond my control, they would tell me there is nothing they can do for me, then hang up. This time around there's no question in my brain that calling them would only make things worse. A niggling feeling in my gut also screams that the guys aren't necessarily safe, either. The person who planted it has to know that I have some sort of relation with the guys or else the effect wouldn't work.

Gargling mouthwash, I slosh it completely around my mouth before spitting it out. The blue liquid slowly spins around the drain, the bubbles popping as it moves down into the pipes and out of sight. So many different thoughts cloud my brain that there's no possible way to cope with how I'm feeling. It's hard to discern what is reality anymore, and at this rate, I wouldn't be opposed to saying this is all one giant hallucination.

Let's be honest, my mental health isn't the greatest right now. So, let's start with that.

Going back into the main room, they managed to set the head on the coffee table and are examining it like a kid would a frog on science day.

"What do you think happened?" Maverick asks as he surveys the head. None of us really know what to say, but my front door is still open, so we can all see the crazy amount of blood that's laying on the doorstep. Of course, my door is above everything else, so it's hard to even get up here without knowing where to go.

"Why would they get someone who looks like you?" I ask also, not really sure what I'm looking at. Well, I will take that back. I know exactly what I'm looking at. A dead guy with his head severed is sitting on my coffee table for Christ's sake. Not like I can ask him what happened or anything.

"Fuck," Ghost curses, backing away several steps. "There's no fucking way we can get out of this alive if..." he looks around at the guys again, all of them obviously on the same wavelength.

"More secrets," I mock with an eye roll. "Anything you want to share?"

"No," Warden spits out the same time Viper says "yes."

"Which is it?" I can't take their back and forth anymore. It's all too much at this rate. "You all are getting far too much for my head right now. First you want me, then you don't, then you do again. What is it going to be?"

"There's a lot of shit you don't know about right now," Ghost mutters, his fingers raking through his hair. I can see the tension rolling off of him in waves. I'm in between wanting to reach out and give him the biggest hug and punching him in the face so hard he blacks out.

"I'm not a fucking child, Ghost," I spit and the effect seems to land on the mark when his fingers swiftly grip my throat. Hands flying to grip his wrist, he walks me backward step by step until I'm pressed against the wall. His glare burns holes into my face as he inspects me closely. My airway isn't cut off, but it's definitely restricted...blood flow restricted, I feel airy and light. The devilish smirk that covers his lips indicates he knows exactly what he is doing to my body. To me.

"Poor Little Pyro," he taunts as his other hand grazes along the shirt on my torso. I can't feel his touch but the soft fabric from the inside is smooth and silky, the exact opposite of the hand that has me pinned around the throat. "You don't know half the demons that want to play with you." Maverick grabs his shoulder and jerks him backward slightly. Ghost doesn't remove his hold on me, yet takes a single step back. Those few inches feel like a weight coming off my shoulders and letting me just breathe a little easier.

"Let's not get carried away," Viper warns Ghost though he's standing beside Maverick and eyeing my body like he wants to take the place of his companion. "She needs to understand what's going on with her life before she starts letting those conclusions rear their fucking heads." Warden stands on the other side of Ghost. He nudges Ghost slightly which seems to be enough for him to finally let go. A large huff exits from him as he takes several steps away from me, his eyes never straying from mine as he moves backward.

"We should head over to the clubhouse," Maverick pitches wisely. The guys all seem to agree with him, yet the thumping organ in my chest doesn't want to stop what Ghost has started. There is plenty of time for chit-chat later. Right now, I'm fucking horny from getting teased and choked. Just as I'm about to protest, Viper grabs the head from the coffee table and throws it in the air like a baseball.

I think I might puke again.

Chapter Seventeen

Regan

We walk down to the alleyway where the four men parked their bikes. Walking over to them, I pick the one I think is the coolest and wait. None of the men move, they stand there and watch me as I take in the bikes. Rolling my eyes, I go to throw my leg over one of them when I'm stopped by Maverick. His fingers reach out, gently moving the stray hairs away from my ears before pulling a full helmet over my head. He brushes back more hair so they don't get caught on the straps.

"Why do I have to wear a helmet but you guys don't?" I sass, yet there is no fire behind the words. So much so that my arms dangle limply at my side and ignore the pressing feeling to shove my fist into his dick.

"I'm carrying precious cargo, so it needs to be protected at all costs." His explanation makes me want to simultaneously vomit and swoon. Not only that, but the warmth in his deep brown eyes captivates me as my heart beats a little harder. It doesn't help that I know they really don't want anything to do with me outside of this. It doesn't take a rocket scientist to know that my presence will be more of a burden on them than they wanted. That's why they were trying to get rid of me. They know I have nothing to really bring to the table besides awful mental health issues. Well, that and an up and coming book store that seems to be doing pretty good.

He continues to do the straps up, and I stand quietly, unable to make a snarky retort back to him. Once the straps are secured tightly below my chin, he inspects the rest of my covered face before nodding to himself. He grabs a face covering from his back pocket and pulls it over his head. It's the same skull style from when they were at the book store all those days ago. I believe they were trying to scare me, but we can see how well that really worked. Straddling the bike, he holds a leather covered hand out for me to grab. I completely ignore it. I grip his shoulder tightly and swing my leg over effortlessly. There may have been a stint of riding a few years ago…I don't wait for his reaction. Nestling close to his back, I wrap one arm around his torso while I rest the other on my thigh. He kicks the stand up and peels out of the alleyway.

It doesn't surprise me, though I can tell from the way his hand grabs mine that he anticipated me to fly off the back of it. With another eye roll, I debate whether I want to tease him or not…

He lays a single hand on my knee while the other lays on the throttle. We fly through town effortlessly as he takes us back to, I assume, the club. Snaking my other arm around his torso, I graze my fingers over his abdomen and twist my pointer finger in his shirt. His thumb drags over my knee in what appears to be him reciprocating the gesture. Fingers going just below his pecs, I dig them deep into his covered flesh and drag down.

When he jolts, I know I have caught him off guard. Giggling to myself, I use one hand to pin him backwards to me and the other to tease the lip of his waistband. A rumble vibrates my breasts, and it spurs me on as I creep further down and cup his jean-clad bulge. Hips jerking forward, he acts taken by surprise as I grip him in my hand. His jaw ticks, the small vein in his neck bulges outward yet he doesn't attempt to stop me. Instead, he rocks forward. Length hardening and pressing against the zipper of his jeans, he pumps himself in my grip. My hold is tight and unwavering as he continues to growl. Feeling invigorated, I rock my own hips against the vibrations from the purring bike between my thighs.

Several moments of his cock growing thicker and thicker in his jeans, his hand moves from my knee and grips my wrist. His jaw flexes and moves, but I can't hear a sound. It's not hard to figure out that he's telling me to stop. A warning. One that I plan on ignoring completely.

Maverick catches me off guard when he takes a sharp corner, the back tire fishtailing slightly as we hit dirt roads. The squeal that squeezes past my lips seems to have made its way to Maverick's ears based on the slight quirk in his cheek. He eyes me from his peripheral vision, though he doesn't do it for long, instead going back to focus on the open dirt road.

I remember reading something when I was younger that riding is dangerous enough on pavement, but when it comes to unstable surfaces, it's a lot harder. My childhood is a giant blur, that much I do remember, though I can recall the time one of the foster parents got his honda out of storage. It was a deep cherry red, he said it was an after-market paint job, and it was shiny. You could easily tell he took good care of it. My fascination grew from there and sprouted into emptiness and loneliness. Foster care was only good when those who were caring for you actually cared. Sighing heavily, I do my best to expel that from my head. Too many emotions are slamming into me today, and seeing the dude's severed head didn't help anything at all.

Lights shine toward us from the distance as street lights finally come into view. Nothing about this seems familiar to me, though a sense of longing fills my chest. Deja vu hasn't struck in a long time, yet this is where I belong.

Too bad those who would make it worth my while aren't willing to keep me. Good thing for them is that I won't force them to keep me for much longer. Being a burden on someone is a mental challenge of itself. I would never traumatize them in seeing my body especially after the whole thing with the head guy. It really put some things into perspective for me. No offing myself for the random person to find me. That's off the table. It has to be planned. Methodical.

Would you live if they asked you?

It's a crazy concept that my subconscious believes my will to live rides solely on these four men. When I accidentally burned down my foster placement's home, I remember vividly the slurs that were thrown my way. The names I was called, the brutal bullying I suffered at the hands of my peers and elders. You would think they would be more compassionate for the teenager who almost died. They aren't compassionate for the teenager who started the fire.

Maverick skids to a stop in front of the well-lit house. Rock music pours loudly from inside of the house. He pushes the kickstand down, and before I can even think about how I'm going to get off, he grabs my waist and pulls me off. Like I weigh nothing at all, he simply sets me on my feet and gets to work taking off my helmet. His fingers graze the straps ever so carefully as he works to unwind the hairs that strayed into the metal clips. Neither one of us says a word as he undoes it. He can't see my face with the visor pulled down, can't see me watching his every movement and facial expressions.

If there is one hint that living is worth it...

Clenching my hands into tight fists, I let the sharp edges of my nails dig into my palms. The skin draws taut as I feel the tell-tale sign of my skin giving way as it opens. Liquid drips down my hand freely, no one sees it. Only I can feel it.

Only I can feel the pain that I suffer every day.

The demons that wrap me in their own fists and bang my head into the floorboards. It's all too much. Bleeding makes them stop. It's like sacrificing myself to them is enough to hold them off, even if it's for a few moments.

My hand is ripped upward by my wrist as Viper glares down at me through his skull mask. My pussy flutters with need at the fire in his eyes, but it takes me a minute to analyze his anger until I realize what he sees looking at my bleeding hand.

"Oops," I sigh while attempting to wiggle free from his hold. He doesn't let go, only grips my wrist even tighter. "I didn't mean to hurt myself, I was just trying not to flinch." The lie is poor. Viper can easily see through the bullshit I spew but doesn't comment on it.

"You don't get to make yourself bleed," he hisses as Maverick finally rips the helmet off my head. Maverick inspects the cuts on the hand Viper is holding, then grabs my other hand and looks over that one too. "If you want to bleed, you tell *us*. We *own* you, Little Pyro. If you want to draw blood, we will do it for you."

Chapter Eighteen

Viper

Blood droplets cascade from her hands onto the dark gravel below us. Several seconds go by as I just watch splash on the rocks, absorb into the dirt and leave a small wet spot. I hopped off my bike seconds before she was hoisted off Mav's, and when I clocked her, I saw the way her fingers dug into her palms. It's a coping mechanism. From what? No clue, but it's a common one. When her fingers flexed and finally broke skin, she didn't even flinch. My cock twitched in my jeans. We already knew that she was a bit of a masochist, but my mind swirls with new possibilities of how far we could push that pain boundary.

Snatching her hand up, I inspect the pooling blood on her palm. The light pink mixes beautifully with the red as it travels through the divots of her skin. I can feel her eyes staring at me from behind the visor. Lust and anger radiate through my body at her self-mutilation. "You don't get to make yourself bleed. If you want to bleed, you tell *us*. We *own* you, Little Pyro. If you want to draw blood, we will do it for you." Mav yanks her helmet off her head and stares at her other hand, disappointment emanating from his gaze. Smirking, I lift the bottom of my mask over my nose, bring her hand to my mouth, and lick the salty iron liquid off her hand. She gasps as I lap at her palm, the smooth skin teasing my tongue. Thighs rubbing together, she subtly bounces from foot to foot to gain friction. Sharing a side glance with Mav, I suck her pinky finger into my mouth. Another surprised gasp mixes with a moan as I suck her finger clean. I repeat the process with the other four digits.

"Fuck, Viper," Ghost groans from behind us. Flicking my gaze toward him, he fists himself through his jeans. "Is that how you're going to suck my cock? Lapping at it like a good fucking boy?"

Grinning, I pop her thumb out of my mouth and do one last lick over her entire palm. The bleeding has subsided, but the dark craving in my bones thrums heavily. Looking at my brothers, they all seem to feel the exact same way as I do.

If she wants to bleed, we will make her bleed.

Maverick doesn't clean her other hand off, instead lacing his fingers with hers as blood coats them both, and he drags her behind him. Warden follows closely behind the two not batting an eye, but Ghost has other plans for me. His hand snakes around my throat and hauls me against him. Cock digging in my ass, he grinds himself into me while he applies more pressure to my neck. Air gets harder and harder to enter my lungs, but I don't fight him. If anything, I welcome the slight suffocation. My head grows light as a guttural moan escapes us both. Grabbing the bottom of my mask, he rips it off my head and reveals my messy hair.

"Let's go," he growls in my ear, his hand letting me go and shoving me forward. Grinning, I make my way inside the club. Mav and Regan are stopped inside the door while she takes in the scenery. Can't say that I really blame her either because there are members and jacket pickers fucking on the tables. A sight for sore eyes because I feel at home again. It's been a few weeks since we have been to the club, and seeing them going at it like usual makes the unsettled feeling in my chest diminish just slightly.

Nudging them forward, Regan shoots me a glare as I pass her. Mid fuck, guys raise their hands in salutes before going back to pounding the girls. Some of them sound fake while others sound like they are in utter bliss. Mav leads Regan toward the back room where I have my set up. It's technically my bedroom, but I moved in with Ghost and we use that as our own little playroom. Digging my keys from my pocket, I observe Regan curiously watching me from the corner of my eye. Once the door is shoved open, her jaw drops.

"Holy sex dungeon," she mutters. Ghost and I smirk at her while Mav cackles.

Walls black as the thrumming organ in my chest, the red LED lights barely illuminate the room to keep the shroud of darkness. There's hardly any color in the room besides the occasional red vinyl padding of an implement.

Suddenly serious, I walk up to her and cradle her face in my hands. "Do you trust us?" It's a loaded question because I would not trust me either. But the way she's eyeing me has me rethinking everything. After a moment, she nods. "If there is something you do not like, you don't power through it. While I know you're a masochist, there is a level of trust here."

Confusion morphs in her features, and I wrack my brain for better ways to explain it to her. I'm suddenly bumped out of the way as Warden takes my place. Hands landing on her shoulders, he stares down at her seriously.

"Red means you want everything to stop. Yellow means it is getting a little too intense but you're okay, you just need to change what we are doing. Green means you are good to keep going." She doesn't say anything as her gaze flicks between his eyes. "What are the colors?"

"Green, yellow, red. Green means good, yellow means slow down, red means stop everything." Pride swells at the quick learning of our girl.

"What if we are doing something you don't particularly like, but you're not in pain?" Ghost asks from next to me, catching her attention.

"Depends. If I don't like it at all, I would yellow it and explain if I can. If I'm indifferent to it, then green." Her shoulders shrug as Warden shakes his head with a smirk.

"You will make a great cock slut for us, Little Pyro." Her eyes widen, as she inhales sharply. Smacking her ass, she jolts forward and glares at me.

"Five minutes, you will be on the bed, *naked*, with your ass in the air and your breasts on the sheets," I demand, her head nodding rapidly to agree. *Tsk*ing, I shake my own. "For this to work, you have to use your words like a big girl."

Rolling her eyes, she sighs. "Yes." Quirking a brow at her, I grin.

"You want to try that again?" I ask like she is a petulant child. The disdain on her features lets me know that she's about had enough. Good thing she will be taught how to behave.

"Yes sir," she says without any emotion. Oh, we are going to have fun. Turning on my heel, I motion for the others to follow behind me and leave her behind. One last look over my shoulder, and she's scowling. Not able to contain my laugh, it bursts out of me as the door slams behind us. Setting the timer on my phone, I shove it back in my pocket.

"Hopefully this doesn't push her too far," Mav mutters like the usual worry-wart that he is. Nibbling on his bottom lip, I reach my hand out and release it.

"She will be fine. Regan is a big girl, and there's no way that we will make her do something she isn't ready for." The words leave my lips but they are a slight lie. My mind is made up that we will push her to her limits, then continue to push until she breaks. She is *ours* to break and there will be no one to stand in the way of that.

"What if she doesn't like something but is too afraid to say something?" He questions again, and I swear my blood boils at his dumb questions. The man talks like we didn't fuck her in the tunnels not even a few days ago. She admitted to overhearing us talk about leaving her behind.

"That girl," I point to the door, "is tougher than she looks and the lack of credit you give her is more than disheartening. She wants this whether she says she does or not. Fuck, she saw that dude's head on her table and laughed. Yeah, she puked for a few minutes, but if that's the worst that is going to happen then we are fine."

He nods, taking a deep breath. "Did anyone tell her that 'no' doesn't work?"

"Nope, and we are not going to." Even Ghost looks surprised when Warden answers. He rolls his own eyes, an incredulous look splaying his features. "Viper and I already warned her of the rules and system. She knows exactly what to say to make it stop."

It's like the universe knows I'm done with this conversation, my timer goes off.

Chapter Nineteen

Regan

The door shuts behind them and I swear the blood drains from my body. Quickly stripping out of my clothes, I work fast to do what they have asked. They didn't ask me to braid my hair but others would braid theirs without asking. With a quick curse to myself, I weave my fingers through my hair then realize I don't have a tie. There's no time left for me to worry about it, so scrambling onto the bed I lay my face in the cold sheets and bring my knees under me. The air in the room has a slight chill to it, my flesh rising with goosebumps. Between the cool air and the cold sheets, my nipples pucker and rub precariously with each move I make. I do my best to remain still, but it's a lot harder than I anticipated. That, and the timer should be done—

"Oh look," the southern drawl is distinguishable now. The door is silent on its hinges as the men trail in. "Our Little Pyro is on her knees for us. Her pussy lips are so wet I can see them glistening from here." Stifling the groan, I wiggle my hips a little to build friction and taunt them. Two hands roam over my back as one settles between my shoulder blades. I'm pushed even further into the sheets, my chest being smashed in the soft mattress.

"This would be a perfect spot for my boot," the deep baritone of Ghost's voice sends shivers wracking down my spine. More pressure on my shoulders and I can quickly deduce who is touching me. "Those scabs have healed fairly nicely, too bad we will have to open them back up and make them scar." I go to ask him what he means, but the words never leave because another set of calloused hands skim over my bare ass gently. It's an act, I know, but I want to savor the soothing feeling for a few moments. A single finger dips between my folds and hooks inside of me. Air seizes in my lungs as the digit is removed. Unable to look over at the male, the guttural growl reverberating around the room is clearly Warden.

"You're already soaking wet for us," Warden growls, then something sharp bites me on the ass. Literally.

"Shit!" I curse loudly, unable to contain my surprise. Lips gently kiss the spot and lap at the skin. It's hot, the raw skin cooling as he continues to lick at my ass.

"Naughty words coming from such a good girl," Viper coos as he comes into view. Tucking a stray strand of hair away from my face, he wraps his hand around my long brown hair. I'm not prepared for him yanking my head back as Ghost keeps me pinned to the bed. Maverick stands next to Viper with a long black thing in his hand and a wicked smirk on his face.

He must see the question on my features because he explains. "You want to hurt so much, you want pain? This is a wax candle. When *I* am ready, I will light this up and let the hot wax coat your entire body. Front and back." There's no protest from me, but there's a little niggling worry in the back of my head that I'm quick to shut down.

Mav nods over at Warden then two fingers are shoved deep inside of me. I lurch forward, my eyes slamming closed as he withdraws them and pushes them in again. Over and over, he finger fucks me toward an orgasm. He hits a spot inside of me that feels foreign, and I can't tell if it's a good thing or a bad thing.

"Oh god, I'm going to come," I gasp just as the fingers are ripped out of me. My mistake was announcing my impending bliss instead of asking for it. Oopsie daisy.

Before I can apologize for my mistake, a hand is slamming down on my pussy and the *smack* is mixed with my wetness. My body reaction confuses my head reaction because I drop my hips to be closer to the pussy attacker. My brain screams at me to get away from him. Either way, a moan is what ends up coming out of me because it's still blissful to walk the edge. They are going easy on me. This is just a warm-up for all of us, I know it.

"You do not get to come until we say you can, do you understand me?" Viper's face is inches from mine, his minty breath wafting across my cheek as I attempt to nod in his strong hold. He tightens his fist, stopping me all together with a quirk of his brow.

"Yes sir," I gasp as my air comes in my pants. Nodding, my head is dropped onto the mattress as Maverick comes closer with the candle. I don't know when he was able to light it, but it's suddenly pooling at the tip.

"Now," one of the guys, I can't tell who, demands as Maverick reaches out his hand and pours a splash of the hot wax on my ass. My face scrunches against the heat of the wax, but it wasn't as bad as I had anticipated it to be. Yeah, it was hot, yet it didn't burn. It actually felt good. So good that I can feel my cum dripping from between my thighs.

"She fucking liked that," Viper laughs and the guys join him. Face heating, I know I'm not supposed to be embarrassed, yet I feel it. I don't get a lot of time to think about it before another set of slashes land on my back while more fingers are shoved into my opening. A breathless scream releases from me as my eyes roll back.

"Her mouth needs to be filled, don't you think, Mav?" Viper eyes Maverick out of my sight, and I can't stop the nod.

"Yes, please fill my mouth," I practically sing. Viper works the button of Maverick's jeans and pulls his cock from its confines. From this angle, it's hard to swallow my saliva, so it drips onto the dark sheets and pools by my mouth. It simply shows how much I want their cocks in my mouth. The fingers in my pussy halt as cold liquid drips on my back hole. Panting, I suddenly feel overly full as a single finger is pushed into me. There's no pain, only a slight stretch as I'm filled in both openings.

"You will take our cocks like the good whore that you are," Maverick hisses as he rubs the thick head of his cock against my outstretched tongue. Flicking my tongue against it, he groans as he flexes his bicep. Another harsh splash meets the middle of my spine where the flesh is far too sensitive. He takes that moment to shove himself deep into my throat. Eyes rolling closed, I simply *feel*.

My ass is being stretched with another digit while my cunt takes more fingers than I think can fit on a single hand. Wax moves from dripping onto my back and migrates to my ribs. Another set of hands drags through the warm wax, smearing it along my body. There's no telling right from left, up from down, me from them. We are all one right now, and the thoughts of not existing seem to silence themselves.

"This ass will stretch so nicely for us," Viper hisses as a hand cracks down on my ass. Moaning around Maverick's cock, he shutters and stills.

"I'm going to come if you keep that shit up," he grunts loudly before pulling out. Viper takes his place, mounting next to my head and sliding home. His heavy balls slap the mattress as he pumps into my mouth ruthlessly. The hand pressing into me disappears along with the numerous fingers plugging me. Emptiness sets in my lower region but the fire stokes higher with each wicked drop of wax.

"She's fucking covered," one of them taunts, and with the lack of senses, there's no telling who that would be. My back is up in flames from the constant heat and pressure, but thankfully they don't make me wait long for more.

Something rough lands between my shoulders again as a cock notches itself at my opening. Eyes snapping open, I don't have time to process the heavy shove on my back and cock slamming into me. Garbled words echo out of me as I struggle to contain myself. Viper's cock keeps me fairly quiet as, I assume, Ghost pounds into me from behind. Someone winds my hair in the fist and hoists me onto my hands, knocking the boot away from my back.

Two men, Viper and Warden, push their cocks together and attempt to slide into my mouth. Absolutely no way they are going to fit but they try. Both backup slightly as they decide to take turns. Blood whooshes in my ears as the thrusting from behind picks up, my pussy burning with need. So much is happening, but there isn't enough to tip me over the edge.

I know my body, and I have never come without clit stimulation. It doesn't help that I have only ever had one lousy fuck, but tit-for-tat. A hissing sound that resembles fire being put out hits my ears before another body joins us on the bed.

"Wax coming off is going to hurt like a fucking bitch," Ghost laughs as someone picks at the hardened stuff on my back. He wasn't joking. Like someone has doused my skin in fire and is trying to peel it off the bone, the pain radiates to my entire body. A slight shriek slams out of me when a giant area is ripped off. Tears well in my eyes at the sheer pain, but each time he slams into me while the wax is ripped away, my orgasm inches closer. I'm riding the fine line between pain and pleasure, yet all I want to do is scream into the abyss while floating away in my head.

Light and airy, my mind slowly drifts away from this land. The pain is still there ever so subtly, but I don't really feel the pain anymore. If anything, my pleasure ramps up tenfold when something caresses my clit and vibrates with abandon. The cock from my mouth is ripped away, and I scream.

"Yes!" Ghost shouts as he slams into me two more times. "Fuck, come all over my fucking cock like the little cock whore you are!" I do exactly as he asks, taking it as my permission to let go. Shrieking my release, I swear something from my lower region sprays over him. Not really caring, my orgasm rolls over me in a multitude of shock waves. Emptiness quickly follows before I'm plugged closed again. This time, something breaches my ass at the same time a cock slams home. Higher and higher I fly with each plunge of a man inside of me. Feeling far too full, my stomach rolls as Maverick slams his cock down my throat making me gag. Vomit threatens to come back up with each thrust, but they are far too punishing for it to escape.

"My fucking turn," Warden shoves Maverick out of the way as he forces me to swallow all of him. Not wanting him to get the upper hand, I do my damndest to make eye contact with him. His striking blue eyes threaten to do more than drown me in the pools of his abyss, the tattoos over his chest move with every thrust. One of his arms flies up to grip something above his head when I see what appears as a grim reaper. I don't have the capacity to think it over too much before his wicked smirk drags me back into the feeling of overstimulation. Maverick's large hand grips Warden's hair, yanking his head back, and whispering something in his ear. Whatever is exchanged makes Warden pick up his pace in my throat. Whoever is behind me follows the rhythm of the other. Maverick's bicep is on display, and he has the same tattoo.

Suddenly, cocks all disappear from me and I'm flipped onto my back. The niggling thoughts are back as my entire body is on display for them. None of them seem to care as Warden and Ghost grip my ankles and bend me in half while Viper lines himself at my entrance and slides home.

"One of these days," he growls, getting nose to nose with me, "you will take two of us in the tight cunt while you take one of them in your tight asshole. Whoever is left will have to fuck that mouth of yours, keep it plugged so it can't talk back." A white vibrator is suddenly brought between my thighs and lands directly on my clit. There's no holding back.

I scream as white stars slam into my vision, the air in my lungs completely expelling as I come harder than I have in my life. My fingers and toes are numb as my limbs shake. Breathing becomes a chore, my mind is static. "That's right, come for us like a good Little Pyro." Not able to gauge who it is, liquid drips over my stomach before the distinct sound of a zippo pops open. Eyes snapping open, blood and static still overtake my senses though I can see the fire sparking to life. It draws my attention as it burns orange with a blue base. Gaze flitting between Maverick who holds the lighter and the flame itself, I'm completely captivated when he drops it. On me. My first instinct reaction is to move out of the way. I may love fire and have pyro tendencies, but burning myself has never really been on the table. My second reaction isn't one that I would even condone. I moan.

The heat from the fire as it burns over my skin without affecting me. Whatever liquid they poured over me is burning away fast, and the flame is getting hotter and hotter on my skin. Just as I start to thrash, Maverick bends down and blows out the flame.

"Again, please," I rasp. None of us in this room have all of our mental screws tightened, so they agree without hesitation. More liquid, more fire, and I don't think I have ever been this high in my life. Another orgasm rips through me with the fire, but my vision goes from white stars to black spots to complete darkness.

If this is how I die, it's one happy death.

Chapter Twenty

Warden

Lifting her in my arms, she weighs practically nothing. When we were at her apartment, it didn't fail my notice that she didn't have a lot. There didn't seem to be a lot of food in the cabinets. I didn't inspect the fridge, but I can probably guess there isn't going to be much there either. The stupid organ thumping in my chest has me holding her a little tighter to my chest as I take her to my room. Mav follows me silently while Viper and Ghost go to their shared room. Laying her gently on the bed, she stirs briefly then settles. She snuggles into the pillow with one arm splayed out under the pillow. Leg straight, her other one L's next to her body. The red wax on her back is caked on her in thick globs, and when I look over at Mav, he's grimacing.

"At least her brand is healing fine," I mutter in an attempt to lighten his mood a little. He nods as he inspects the beginning of the bruises on her back from the wax that we pulled off. After several moments of silence, Regan makes a choking sound. Mav and I both stop moving, practically stop breathing as her hips start to gyrate against the bed. Smirking over at Mav, he just shakes his head at me. He leans over her sleeping, moaning form, kisses her hair then leaves.

I don't have that level of restraint.

Feet taking me to her face, her expression appears to be in utter bliss. With the way she's rubbing her thighs together and tilting her hips, I would say she's trying to get herself off. Leaning down, I brush the stray hairs out of her face. Her brows are furrowed, cheeks bright red, puffy lips popped open as she moans softly in her sleep.

As silently as I can, I crawl onto the bed and position myself by her naked lower half. Her soft thighs are covered in marred white raised scars, and it takes me a second to realize they are self-mutilation scars. Rage burns in my gut, especially when Viper warned her that her blood is *ours*. They look old, so I can't be too angry at her, yet it needs to be pounded into her that she is *ours* to mutilate and make bleed.

Unbuttoning my jeans again, my cock comes out easily. I'm hard, ready for her sweet cunt to swallow me. I wasn't able to get into her earlier, but that isn't going to stop me.

As gently as I can to keep her from waking, I graze my free hand over her bumpy skin and admire the strength she has. She is a warrior from her own mind. I let my hand wander to her folds and gently part them to see a mixture of cum at her entrance. Admiring it, I grip my cock harder in my fist. She doesn't move as I let my thumb graze over her swollen clit. Rolling it in slow circles, her moans turn breathy as she moves with each circle. My fingers dip into her sweet cunt and scoop the cum mixture, I use it as lubricant for my cock to get me wet. Notching myself at her entrance, I push into her slowly. Her hands ball into fists, one of them gripping the sheets tightly as I pump into her.

"Warden," she moans breathlessly, and I freeze. Her eyes remain closed, her body still humping me as I stay still. With the way her hips are moving, she's fucking herself on my cock like a pro. It takes everything in me to not groan in pleasure as my balls tighten, threatening to come here and now.

The door swings open and Mav stops in his tracks. He shakes his head but enters, shutting the door behind him. Walking toward us, he admires the way she fucks herself on me as I hold onto the last bit of sanity I have. He eyes where her cunt meets my cock, and with his own smirk, reaches forward and trails his fingers over her clit.

"I'm next," he whispers and all I can do is nod. He rubs circles furiously over her clit as she moves faster on me. A growl of approval catches in my throat as her pussy clenches around me, a shriek of pleasure falling from her sleeping form as she comes. My teeth clench tightly in my mouth as the urge to make her bleed rushes through me. The need to bite into her perfectly marred flesh settles into me. Mav must see my struggle as he throws his wrist in front of my face. Clamping onto his wrist, I immediately spit out his hairy ass arm. He chuckles quietly then nods at me. Fingers clamping on her hip, I slam into her over and over again before letting go. My cum floods her tight channel as she pulses around me and Mav watches her face for any signs of consciousness. Still, she remains unfazed from dreamland.

With a wicked smirk, I slowly pull out of her and change spots with Mav. He moves swiftly, not hesitating to shove inside her harshly. She whimpers, hand rooting around on the sheets for something. I go to move back but she is quick to latch onto my cock. She fists my softening length in her hand as she mumbles words that are hard to make out.

"Oh Maverick, fuck me harder," she whimpers softly, brows furrowed in pleasure as Mav does as she asks. Dropping his hands to grab her outstretched leg, he pummels into her like she might disappear.

"Fuck, I'm going to flood your pussy, mark you like the good fucking property you are." Mav is quiet as he sneers his declaration over her body, though his eyes soften a smidge after he says it. We are all muddled with thoughts about what we are going to do with her to get our mission completed.

"Own her cunt," I hiss at him as I bring him back to the present. He returns it with a wild grin, then buries himself to the hilt.

"She's choking my cock," he sputters while sliding into her quickly and pulling out slowly.

"I'm going to come," Regan sighs, and my fingers pick up speed on her clit. His fingers dig into her thigh hard enough to bruise and he roars his release, not bothering to remain silent. Her eyes finally pop open for a split second as she squirts all over his lower half before her eyes roll to the back of her head

Chapter Twenty-One

Ghost

Viper and I sit quietly on the bed in our room, his head on my shoulder while we both try to process what we are going to do. My words have already come back to bite me in the ass. There was an instant connection with her when we tried to scare her off that very first day where her eyes met all of ours head-on. She didn't flinch, didn't stutter as she continued on with her grand opening. It's like she knew her strength and played into it.

"Quit beating yourself up," Viper mumbles as his lips rest against my shoulder. Unable to help myself, I roll my eyes.

"I should have known that shit would come back at me." The penance in my tone has Viper straightening, his brows furrowed in confusion.

"You are acting like we all didn't have a part to play in this," he starts, holding his hand up when I open my mouth in protest. "Shark told us directly that we either have her on board or give her the boot. For her safety, we wanted to give her the boot. Now, I don't foresee that being much of a choice. She's made it clear that she doesn't want to go, and the guys have not said anything to sway away from that thinking process."

"Ghost, let's make one thing clear, she *wants* this. To be honest, I think she knows what being involved with us entails. We need to be placing our focus on the ring that Shark told us about. The guys know we are running out of time and arrangements need to be made for her to stay with the club. There are plenty of jobs around the compound that she can do like helping with the kids or helping in the library since that's what she loves. You're stressing way too much over something that is this minor." Sighing, I let Viper cradle my head in his hands.

There's nothing left to say. If anyone were to be with her, this club is the safest. I also know that she is strong and will kick someone's ass if they start fucking with her. We sit in silence for what seems like hours before the door to our room is opened. Mav and Warden both look freshly fucked, and I know they can both see the questioning looks in our gaze.

"We didn't fuck one another if that's why you're looking at us like that," Mav laughs as he runs his fingers through his hair. "I did catch this perv though." Viper and I both look at Warden suspiciously yet no one comments on it.

"Glad we got that out of the way," I start, looking at the other three guys. "Who is going to watch out for Regan while we are gone? We need to figure this out before tomorrow, which is when we are scheduled to leave."

"Shit," Mav curses and fists his hair. "Time has gone far too fast." Nodding, they sit on the couch across from us.

"Who can we trust to watch her?" Viper questions, his face dipping into my throat as he inhales. He's simultaneously soothing both of us.

"Honestly? Any of the guys would be great for her, but I was thinking of entrusting her with Servants of the Sun workers," Warden states as if that's been the plan the entire time. "Think about it, the adoption agency will have plenty of things for her to do and keep her busy while we are not here to play house. She can have tasks that actually make a difference. Not only that but it will also show Shark and the others that she's not a burden on us or the club. Either Servants of the Sun or Alley Katz Clubhouse can use her."

"I mean, she owns a bookstore for fucks sake, that must mean she can read and maybe teach others to read?" Ghost question, gaining a perplexed look from Mav.

"Well, just because someone can read doesn't mean they can teach others how to, but I get your point. I would also assume she has some type of education in English, so we can put her to good use." Mav has a point. It would be one thing to cash in one of our I-owe-you's, or another to actually just have the adoption agency or the group home staff just help her blend it. We aren't planning to be gone for months this go around, so I'm mentally crossing my fingers and toes for an eventful mission.

Grabbing my laptop from the night stand, I power it up and download the information from the hard drive. Four different colored dots pop up on the screen for our region, red being the most predominant.

"This looks targeted to specific age groups," I state, noticing that the youngest ages are the highest involved. "What value do they have to be involved?" The Mountain Range Circuit is about two hours south of us, other MC's in the area are willing to assist if needed, but we are more ruthless. They call us the Blood Reapers for a reason.

"These numbers don't make sense." Viper's tongue clicks as he stares at the screen with me. Mav and Warden can't see the screen, so I grab my travel screen and connect it, giving it to them. Studying the map, they look just as confused as us.

"Projected individuals on the compound are one per one hundred children." Mav is the smartest one of us, that's for damn sure, because the ratio is correct. "If they are infants, that would make some sense because their ability to do anything is zero, however for the teens…it's still the same number. Kids rebel against situations that are negative, and with there being ninety-nine additional teens per one adult, then rebelling should be easy."

An odd thought strikes me, one that I'm not entirely sure makes a whole load of sense. "What if the conditions of the compound aren't awful until they are auctioned?"

"Explain," Warden demands. I shoot him a glare before returning to the other two men.

"Like you said, they would rebel if they aren't happy, so what if the conditions in which they are kept are not necessarily bad? They may be bribed to work or be forced to do things to eat, but what if they are under the impression that it could be far worse?"

"Or, the numbers are skewed and it's a death trap," Viper interrupts, his line of thinking also not too far off but much more disturbing than I would like.

"We don't have time to think about the logistics of ratios and math right now, not even time to argue about it. Regan can wake up at any point and we need to be ready to explain shit to her. Figuring out man-power, I say we go in with the same level of ammo we always do. I refuse to go unprepared for a mission that is avoidable. Other MC's in the area are already scouting the traffic and helping gauge projected numbers to assist in target response." Of course, Maverick is the one to get us back on track. "Get Globe on the phone with Steel MC to figure out if they are willing to help us. Have him reach out to other MC's in the area also, it gets some of the leg work off of us."

"I'm on it," Warden insists, standing up from his spot on the couch and exiting the room with his phone in hand. I continue looking at the map for more clues, but I come up empty.

"Anything else?" I question the remaining men. Neither one of them says anything as they also assess the map. After several more minutes, I can see Mav growing physically irritated.

"Something just isn't adding up but I can't put my finger on it. There's too much happening in this general area that it's hard to place where they are taking them from."

"Globe is looking into it," Warden says as he comes back into the room. "Globe also said that the girls at the adoption agency and group home would love to have Regan join their team, apparently they need someone to help in the library." I nod, trying to come up with the best way for us to tell Regan that she really has no other choice but to stay with us and explain the agencies, however I quickly realize I have never been there.

"Have any of you been to Servants of the Sun or Alley Katz Clubhouse?" I ask and they all shake their heads.

"Shark insisted that we try to keep the club side of things separate from them. Something about not wanting to traumatize children more when they are trying to be rehabilitated and working through their own trauma." Nodding, we all understand that easily. We are a rough group of guys, and while we don't necessarily make the best choices, we do what's best for our future. That includes saving these children from trafficking and using our available funds to get them home or doing something useful with themselves.

"So, who is going to tell Regan?" Mav asks, clapping his hands together.

"Tell Regan what?" Standing in the doorway is a completely naked Regan. Her arms are crossed over her chest, her bruised body on display for us. She's a sight for sore eyes, that's for damn sure. We all eye one another, the confession sitting on the tips of our tongues before shaking it off. If she hasn't figured it out that she is marked permanently as ours now, there's no point in spooking her right before we leave. Compliance is key right now along with her safety. She has to stay for us to be able to keep an eye on her.

Chapter Twenty-Two

Regan

I woke up in a bed that wasn't mine and wasn't Maverick's, so I panicked slightly as I dashed out the door. Standing here as naked as the day I was born, I barely realize that I don't have any clothes on. Obviously it's a little too late, so I straighten my shoulders, cock a brow, and wait for them to answer my question. Instead of answering anything, they just look stunned to see me.

Maverick has a screen on his lap that has several different dots displayed on the screen with the red ones being the majority. Wracking my brain, I try to remember what those meant but I come up blank. They also fail to tell me what exactly they mean when they ask each other who was going to tell me something. If last time didn't mean anything to them, then I don't know if they can ever learn from their stupid mistakes.

"We were trying to figure out who you can hang out with while we are gone," Maverick finally answers once his eyes leave my nipples and meet mine. The deep brown slams against mine as I fail to produce thoughts for a split second. Regaining my composure, I nod.

"And why exactly do I need to stay here?" They all give me incredulous looks. I remember the crazy scenario of the head on my porch, but there are friends' houses I could stay at...well, I could stay with Penelope if she has free couch space.

"With everything going on in our world, you're not safe to be out there by yourself. You're wearing our brand and that alone can put a major target on your back. Literally."

"What do you mean, I'm wearing your brand?" I splay my arms out letting the small rolls of fat droop with gravity. "I'm not wearing anything except skin and wax. Also, I do have cum leaking from my cunt, so that counts as wearing something too." The guys look at one another again like I said something wrong. A gut-deep fire builds as anger slowly rolls through my veins. All four of them have kept me in the dark about so much, and this is *my* life they are messing with. I refuse to be a pawn in my own fucking life!

"You will be working with at-risk youth at Servants of the Sun, the adoption agency that is tied with our club as well as Alley Katz Clubhouse, the group home that is also involved with us," Ghost admits, looking at the other men with a hint of warning I can't decipher. "Why don't you grab some clothes from one of the rooms and we can talk about it more, hmm?" Rolling my eyes at his demand posed as a question, I turn on my heel and sashay down the hall. I can feel their eyes burning holes in my back, and that's totally fine. They can look, but right now, they don't get to touch.

Just have to repeat that seventy times to remember it.

A buttery soft shirt sits on the bed all crumpled up, and I'm immediately drawn to it. Inspecting it closely, I don't see any stains or marks that would make it too dirty to wear. The shirt slides easily over my head and fits loosely around my body. Smiling to myself, I leave the dirty underwear on the floor and trek back to the room. None of them are in there, instead voices trail from further down the hallway. I have no clue about anything within the clubhouse besides the constant noise. It's what woke me up from my amazing dream of orgasms-galore. Turning a corner, I'm frozen by the sight in front of me again. Being honest with myself, I completely forgot that there were men and women fucking like bunnies out in the open. Yeah, I dabbled in riding bikes, but this shit is new to me. Tucking tail and turning on my heel, I attempt to escape back to the room when a hand wraps itself around my wrist.

Not thinking, I immediately grab them back and twist until they fly over my shoulder and land on their back. Some guy with a graying beard lays on the ground panting, a dirty smirk on his face as he stares between my legs.

"Ugh, don't be a dirty dog and tell me who you are," I demand as I drop next to him and press my hand into his throat.

"Ah, I see you have met Haze," another voice announces from behind me. My entire nervous system is on fire as I take in the newcomer. He smiles genuinely, his hands held out in surrender. "I'm Shark, the president. Haze is our secretary. He was *supposed* to be helping you get some clothes from the agency ladies, but I see he has gotten a little...preoccupied." Shark smirks down at his fellow member, shaking his head with disappointed humor.

"Where are my men?" I question, the tone coming out of me is a hell of a lot stronger than I am, that's for sure. My hands shake with nerves as my temper flares the ends of my sanity.

"They had a meeting they needed to attend and asked that we help get you situated. Usually I would make them do it, however they are on crunch time and you're not used to what we have to offer," he explains as I stand and step away from Haze. He assesses me for another moment with a quirky brow. Nodding at him is what must give him the permission he requires because he bounces onto his feet like he is in his early twenties.

"You remind me of my ol' lady." Haze has a laugh that could only be described as hearty. Hand on belly, he's deeply amused by me, I can tell. "Sweet Ulia passed away a few years ago from cancer, but she loved working with the agencies and helpin' them kids get back on their feet. We have been searching for another librarian, ya' know. When the guys said you own a bookstore and were pretty sure you were smart, the auctioneer called 'sold'!" He has a drawl that's similar to Viper's but much different. Maybe more Tennessee-ish? I'm not educated in the geography of accents, so it's quick to escape my brain. His story of his wife latches onto my bleeding heart, though.

"Haze will get you settled in with the girls. Don't worry, they will get you appropriate attire prior to being introduced to any minors. That would be illegal and you would have to be arrested," Shark cackles as he walks away from us. Balking at his receding form, I can't even get onto his level of humor. Maybe it's the confusion for everything going on around me, the quick pace the guys are taking me on as they consume me whole.

"Can you tell me a little more about the agencies?" I ask, deciding that I need to get my mind off the four idiots taking space in my mental rolodex.

"Definitely. So, Servants of the Sun is the adoption agency that we work closely with. Ulia actually helped create it back in the day. It's meant to be the first place children go when they come back from their precarious situations. We do our best to quarantine them and figure out their familial situation. If they don't have any available family, then we look at potential adoption. Sometimes, kids aren't adoptable because of the trauma they've gone through or the overwhelming needs they have. So, while they wait for adoption, they are housed with others at Servants of the Sun. Kiddos who don't have families or are higher-needs stay at Alley Katz Clubhouse. Both agencies have amazing workers that help stabilize the children for their next adventures in life. Some of the current prospects are kiddos that have gone through Alley Katz."

It takes everything in me to not stop in my tracks and listen to him speak. The way he speaks about these two agencies has my heart beating a little faster with happiness.

"So, the club kind of takes the other children under their wing?" I question, wanting to make sure I'm hearing it correctly.

"Pretty much. There are some kids that have stayed until they are eighteen then flew the nest. We did our best, but they were harder to get through than the others. There was speculation on what happened to them, yet the staff just weren't able to get through to them." The happy flutters suddenly turn sad for the children who have lost themselves. Mental health is hard for adults and harder for children. I know their development can be drastically reduced if they are in contact with constant trauma, so it's heartbreaking to know they weren't able to be helped.

"What else is there to know before I show up half-naked?" I joke, and he returns the laugh.

"You pretty much know it all. You will meet the fine ladies and gentlemen that make this world go round while you're there. They are friendly and overly welcoming, so you should blend right in. Maverick mentioned that you are a fan of the quiet, so we made sure to have you well acquainted with the library."

Another wave of calm washes over me. Even though my guys weren't able to be here for me physically, they made sure I'm being taken care of. The darkness in the deep recesses of my mind threaten to rear their ugly heads, but Haze keeps talking which seems to sooth them for a little while longer.

"I can't express how appreciative I am," I start, but he is quick to cut me off.

"Nonsense. While I wouldn't recommend being part of this shit show, you're already far too involved to leave. So, you might as well enjoy it while you can." After that, we walk in silence.

He wasn't joking when he said I am far too involved. Just thinking about the shit that I have overheard isn't fun and games. None of the guys have explicitly expressed what they do for the club or what the club is actually all about. They should know that I'm not dumb and wasn't born yesterday, so I can deduce what's going on around me.

Rounding the corner, I feel like I'm experiencing another wave of pure *awe*. Two huge buildings stand next to one another, and the letters of SOTS on one of the buildings and ALLEY KATZ on the other. Haze must notice my lack of movement after he's already fifteen steps ahead of me because he turns around and laughs at me.

"Impressive, huh?" All I can do is nod. Another laugh, he motions for me to follow him. "Pick up your jaw, you might catch a fly or two." Snapping my mouth closed, I mock glare at him.

Entering the agency isn't any less impressive. The walls are dark green on the bottom and white on the upper half with wood pieces sticking out on the bottom. I don't know the style, but it's elegant while still youthful. There are photos of kids scattering the walls with members of the club, which makes my lips pull into a small smile. While they scowl at the camera, their eyes are another story. Crinkles on the sides of their eyes show that they've laughed, that they were happy taking the photo with the kid as the star.

"You must be Regan!" A short blonde female comes bounding out. A slight shriek is pushed from my lungs as I jump backward.

"Wini, you have to stop doing that!" Haze grumbles as he walks around me. "How are you?" She pulls him into a hug that seems far too big for her small stature. There is no way she's more than five-feet.

"I'm alright, hanging in there. Now move out of the way, you big oaf!" Small but mighty, she practically shoves Haze out of the way to get to me. "I'm Winifred, but most people call me Wini. Haze here mentioned that you would be joining us and asked that we get your wardrobe situated." She eyes me up and down, though there is no malice in her stare.

"Do you need me to twirl or..." she rolls her eyes at me, motioning me to follow her. "I take that as a no."

"Girl, I got you, don't worry your pretty head," she giggles, and I make a mental note to be careful what I say around her. Something about her gives off 'I will cut you if you fuck up' vibes, but also screams 'I'm delicate', if that makes any sense.

"Welcome!" A group of girls scream and rush me.

Fuck me, this is going to be pure chaos.

Chapter Twenty-Three

REGAN

Hands flying over my ears, I recoil from their excitement. I don't think my nervous system can handle this level of noise without proper preparation.

"Ladies!" Haze booms while shielding my body away from theirs. Embarrassment creeps over me at my inability to cope with them. I don't even have any real clothing on, for fuck's sake. Way to make my welcome even more embarrassing. "Y'all know that she's new and needs to get situated. We get you are all excited, but relax and welcome her calmly." The girls all do their own level of grumbling before shoving him out of the way and circling me like they are hungry hyenas.

"Uhm," I pause, gulping in air as my chest threatens to cave. "Hi?"

"This is Mila and Irene. Mila is the head of the counseling center and Irene is the head of case management at the agencies. We wanted to formally introduce ourselves, but I suppose we didn't really think this through." Wini worries her bottom lip between her teeth, looking at the ground shyly. The other two girls, Mila and Irene, both appear to be just as embarrassed as their friend.

Sighing, I tug the ends of the shirt down further to hide my body and smile.

"It's nice to meet you ladies. I don't want to be that person, but can I get some clothes?" It takes me finally asking for Mila to turn on her heel and take off, her cherry red hair swishing behind her. Opening my mouth to call after her, I realize I don't really know her that well. If she's leaving because I upset her, then I'm probably not the most qualified person to be following her to make sure she's alright. Before I can stress it any further, she comes trotting back with a string-style bag on her shoulder that looks heavy.

"Here are some clothes to pick through as well as toiletries. There's not a whole lot, but the guys did try to tell Haze what you wear size wise. Now, it all comes down to Haze actually getting it right." Mila sticks her tongue out at him childishly which results in an eye roll from him. Handing over the bag, she takes several steps back to stand in the group of females. Irene doesn't say anything as she assesses me, and I will admit it's making me slightly uncomfortable. They are all so different, though. Heights vary, hair colors are different, their styles are mis-matched with one another yet they all seem...close.

"Thank you," I mumble shyly before Irene points to a bathroom just down the hall. Not waiting to be excused, I scurry away with my metaphorical tail tucked between my legs.

Slamming the door to the single stall bathroom was an accident, but I don't let it phase me. Uncharacteristically, I dump the bag on the ground and swallow deep gulps of air. I didn't need to see their eyes to know they were judging me. There is not a whole lot left to the imagination when it comes to my body, and the fact that the guys allowed me to go out of their rooms looking like this...

The fire burning in my stomach is stoked with the thought of them just upending my entire life. None of this makes any sense, and I blame myself for knowing that this could end badly. Clenching my fists is the only way I keep from sending my fist through the mirror. It's not the greatest feeling in the world, but it could be worse.

Laughing mirthlessly at myself in the mirror, I can't stop the tears of agony that roll down my cheeks. Too many emotions are running through my body. Fire usually settles me down, entraps me in the snare to keep me calm, but I don't have a lighter nor a place to set one. The need to scream envelops me. Grabbing the bag of clothes, I shove my face into the plastic and let go.

Lungs burn with the effort to remain in control, my own internal fire threatening to overtake me. None of this is uncommon, but the thought of losing control when there is so much at stake around me...

Taking several deep, lungfuls of air, I do my best to lower my heart rate when a knock echoes on the door.

"I will be out in a second," I rasp and try to clear my throat a bit. It doesn't work the greatest, so I don't say anything else.

"It's me." The drawl is all too familiar, and my walls crumble. Tears spring to the backs of my eyes as I open the door. Viper takes in my appearance before herding me back into the bathroom and enveloping me in his strong arms. "What's wrong?" Like the strong woman I am, I crumble into a blubbering mess.

I haven't cried like this in a long time, and while I would like to admit that I am a lot stronger than this, there's a piece of me that finds this slightly healing. He pets the back of my hair gently, his fingers combing the ends as he stands silently. Quite frankly, I didn't take him as the coddling type, yet here he is.

"You want to talk about it?" He questions, I shake my head almost immediately. Instead of asking more of me, we simply stand there silently. Well, if you consider me drying my tears on his shirt, then yeah, that's quiet. Kissing the top of my head, he detaches himself from my death grip. "Get dressed and come back out. You're going to love this place." The smile on his lips seems misplaced, but the gesture is all that matters. His presence soothed something inside of me which causes more error of confusion for my brain.

He doesn't give me time to acknowledge him as he turns around and exits the bathroom.

Chapter Twenty-Four
Viper

My boots land on the table at the same time that Mav shoves them off. Grumbling under my breath about everyone being stuck up, he just laughs at me.

"Looking over this area, it seems there are several locations in which the factory could be running," Globe says from his place behind the massive monitors. When we set this meeting up, he asked for us to come to the monitor room. I can see why. "Titan, the prez from Stallions of Steel, has graciously offered their assistance when you get down there. Their tech guy is working on getting feeds for the most likely areas, but I should warn you, it will be a man-hunt." I'm not the only one internally groaning. There is a lot of fun in hunting someone down, the thrill of the chase is enough to have me in my own version of subspace. Yet the idea of having to take several people on a man-hunt with us has me wanting to cancel this damn mission. I know that's not allowed, but fuck if I'm not tempted.

"How many people are we anticipating needing to bring?" Mav asks, plopping down next to Globe.

"I believe Titan told Shark that they had vans ready, but I would confirm it with him if I were you." He gives Mav a pointed look while pushing his glasses up his nose with a finger in the middle. I want to roll my eyes, but I manage to contain myself. Mav glances over at Warden who nods before pulling his phone out and stepping away.

Sighing, I lean forward with my elbows landing on my knees and head resting in my hands. "Do the numbers accurately reflect the missing children?" All three remaining guys looked at me like I said something crazy. "What?"

Mav shakes his head like he's clearing out some weird thought. "You just sounded really smart." Sneering at him, he cackles at my irritation.

"I say smart shit sometimes, douche receptacle." His brows dip slowly, but obviously decides to brush off the odd diss.

"They have vans, but I vote we bring a few of our own," Warden strides back into the room texting away on his phone.

Globe continues moving things around on his computer screens, codes and numbers flying around on the screen. The colored dots that we have come to know start moving around with lines attached to them. "Missing children come from these areas, and we think they may be with this circuit."

"We need to get packed up and ready to go." Mav slaps his hands on his knees before standing. Giving Globe a pat on the back, he leaves. We file out after him, my confusion even more imminent. Usually, the club is a lot more prepared for things, at least I think.

This is one of the first missions we are officially heading, and I admit that the rest of us have taken a bit of a step back to let Mav lead. He's our Sergeant at Arms for a reason, it would make less sense to have him not be where he is now. As his Enforcers, we follow his lead. He says jump, we ask how high. Some have called us a pack, but honestly, we are just brothers.

As a group, we walk back to the rooms in silence. Branching off with Ghost, he flops on the bed and his arm rests over his eyes with a sigh. I suppress a laugh at his dramatics then lay down next to him. Cuddling into his side, he pulls me closer. "Why do I feel like we are abandoning her?" He is so quiet that I almost don't hear him. "This shouldn't feel like goodbye, but the way my heart is pressing against my chest...I don't know if she will be here when we get back."

"Hey," I whisper as I bring myself up onto an elbow. "Where is this coming from?"

"I have this foreboding feeling that shit isn't right." I don't know how to answer it, so I lay there without another word. After a few silent moments, he starts talking again. "It's a gut feeling that I can't explain. I'm a grown ass man, and I sound like a fucking bitch for saying that my gut is talking to me that isn't I.B.S.." The arm resting over his head moves as his fingers dig into his hair and pull. Grabbing them with my own, I rip them from the strands and tangle his fingers in mine.

"We will figure it out, man," I encourage, though I know Ghost's gut instinct is never wrong. From my recollection, he hasn't been forthcoming with his 'gut feelings' before, but he has warned us away from things before they happened. Unfortunately for us now, that's not something we can do. This mission has to take place whether we have a gut feeling or not. We just have to make sure we get *all* of our bases covered, that includes ensuring the amount of man-power we need is sufficient in the event of a bust.

Opening my mouth to respond, my phone rings. I immediately hit the ignore button. "There are lots of-" Again, my ringtone blares. With an eye roll, I declined the call. If I don't have the person saved, I don't like answering. There are far too many jacket pickers in this place who just want to fuck for the cut. "There are a lot of different ways we can-" More fucking ringing.

"You should probably answer that if they've called three times." Irritation blooms in my chest as I answer the phone.

"What?" I snap on the other end.

"Seriously, you don't have my number saved, jackass?" Looking down at the phone 'Haze' is on the screen. Groaning inwardly, I apologize quickly. "Shut the fuck up and get your ass to Servants of the Sun."

Bolting upright, my breath catches in my throat at the thought that something might have happened to the kids there. "What's wrong?"

"Your girl is having an episode of some kind, I think. I heard a soft scream from her a second ago and now it's quiet. Knocking didn't work, and the girls are looking for the key to the bathroom."

"I'm on my way." Hanging up the phone, I jump from the bed and don't give a backward glance.

"Viper, what happened?"

"Something's wrong with Regan." The stairs seem to be so damn tall now that I need to move down them quickly. Shuffling follows me, but that's the least of my worries. Why the fuck would they have called me? The idiots must not have answered because I'm probably the worst person out of them. Shit, Ghost's phone didn't even vibrate, I don't think. So, why would they call me? Did she ask for me?

Scatterbrained as all hell, I practically sprint to the adoption agency where they said she is. Haze leans against the front counter, the girls behind it as they watch with worried gazes. "She went in there about fifteen minutes ago, but hasn't come out. They slightly harassed her before letting her change." Something deep in my soul is reaching out to the broken girl behind that door. She might not realize it, but I have picked up on her slight body discomfort. She will pick her nails or twirl the bottom of her hair when she's nervous, subconsciously she will move her hands in front of her stomach and legs when we stand there. I have no clue if *she* even realizes that she does it, but I notice. That's all that matters right now.

Giving the three girls a slight glare, I go over to the bathroom and wait. It's silent, far too quiet for my liking when he told me not even five minutes ago that she was screaming. With a deep breath in and out, I knock. Nothing happens for a second, then she tries to shoo me away. The rasp in her voice is awful. Her pain is calling to mine like a savage love song. On one hand, I want to destroy her and build her into something indestructible. On the other, though, I want to protect the perfect girl that she is now, guide her to be the best version she can be because I know what it's like once the fire takes over. Veins no longer get cold with fear or worry. You live for the chase, the thrill of life and the boundaries you can cross. I want to protect my little pyro at all costs.

"It's me." Another few moments of silence, then like someone above does possibly exist, the door unlocks and cracks open just slightly. She looks...beautiful. Her cheeks are bright red from the force of not crying, her body worn and tired from a multitude of excursions that she has gone through. Even I can see the bone deep exhaustion that threatens to overtake her, yet here she is.

Our Little Pyro.

As soon as the words are out of my mouth, I know her facade will crumble. "What's wrong?" Tears go from welling in her eyes to streaming down her cheeks. Without another word, I cradle her closely to my body. Chest tightening, there is nothing for me to do besides letting her get it out. I want to burn the world for her, light everything on fire to make sure there is a clear path when one is needed. The shitty feeling amplifies when she suddenly sniffles and tries to push me away. I don't let her, instead I brush my fingers through the ends of her hair.

That doesn't do any good for her resolve as she melts back against me. Shushing her quietly, I try again. "Do you want to talk about it?" She shakes her head rapidly, and it brings a light smile to my face. I didn't think she would want to, but I figured I would ask anyway. Her hair smells like my shampoo when I lean down to kiss her head which only makes my insides hotter for her. "Get dressed and come back out. You're going to love this place." I don't let her argue with me as I back out of the bathroom and shut the door behind me.

"Is she okay?"

"What's wrong with her?"

"Is she not feeling well?"

I'm bombarded with three worried looking brothers who hammer me with different questions regarding her wellbeing. Holding up both hands, they stop.

"She's alright, just overwhelmed, I think. Once she gets changed, we will walk her around ourselves." Three girls stand off to the side nervously. I haven't spent any time over here because Shark insists that we have to keep our space to not confuse the kids. That, and this is their territory, not ours.

"I think we overwhelmed her," the blonde one with big glasses says softly. She looks so...soft. Almost like she's about to cry, too. Her crying isn't for me, though. Only one female I can deal with crying, and she is currently getting dressed.

"We will show her around and get her settled in, don't worry about it." Of course Mav is the one to step up. He gives Haze a nod of dismissal, and the older man takes it without complaint. Silence is met once the doors shut behind him, none of us speaking as we wait for our girl. After what feels like hours, Regan finally opens the door to the bathroom and shuffles out. Deep set exhaustion coats her face as the sound of her feet drag against the hardwood flooring.

"Little Pyro." Mav swoops toward her, enveloping her in his arms as his mouth drops to the cleft of her ear. The exchange is silent between the two, her eyes twinkling with mirth then she nods. Holding her out from his body, he does one quick assessment before Warden shoves him out of the way to do his own. Mav rolls his eyes but doesn't say anything while Warden scans her over completely. Ghost is next, cradling her head between his large hands while he takes in her shrunken appearance. I wonder if this is what the stress of being around us is like? Shit, it's only been four days yet there's an ageless look about her that has me on edge. She turns to me and takes a step in my direction. Holding out my hand, I grasp hers tightly in mine before motioning for the big glasses girl to lead the way.

"Like I said earlier, I'm Wini. I am the head of Psychiatry here at Servants of the Sun." My brows shoot upward into my hairline. The chick looks smart, but a whole ass mental health person? Remind me to stay at least thirty feet away from her. The other guys look just as concerned as I do. Regan bursts out into a fit of laughter after she catches the color draining from our faces in fear. None of us need to be analyzed. We know we are fucked in the head, don't need someone to tell us that too.

"We have three different wings in this facility, then a different building for the actual group home." Mila takes the lead, motioning for us to follow her down a massive hallway. "Wing Alpha, also known as 'A', is for children ages zero to ten. Wing Bravo, 'B', is for eleven to seventeen. Wing Charlie, 'C', is ages eighteen and up. Once they are eighteen, we mainly work with them for independence and stuff, though we usually try to get them integrated into the club before then. Sometimes the kids we pick up have been in their system for a while and just need a level of structure, so they stay in C until there's room in the club or one of the sister clubs to send them to." That's a lot of information that I didn't know, and again based on the looks from the guys, I believe they didn't know that either.

"Some of the prospects are kids who came from here," Irene says, looking ahead but not at anyone else. She appears colder than the other two, her gaze never straying away from in front of her. "I went through here not too long ago, and it was one of the best programs I could have received. That's why I chose to work here when I aged out of the program."

"We appreciate you being here," Mav says softly, nodding to her in respect. She glances over at him, returns the nods before turning away from his gaze. Awkward silence takes over again as we continue walking down a large hall.

"Through that door is Alley Katz, the group home," Mila says excitedly, pointing at the door. "That's my domain, and my office is the first one on the right when you go through the second set of glass doors." Mila pins Regan with a knowing look, one that I am not privy to, and Regan nods as if she understands the silent conversation. At least one of us knew what was happening. Mila goes through the double doors and points again at her office before continuing to walk.

"You said I would be working in the library?" Regan asks quietly, her eyes sad and tired. "Did they tell you that I own a bookstore?"

"Actually, they did! I wanted to talk to you about seeing if we can set up some of our more responsible youth to help out there for volunteer hours," Mila beams brightly at a surprised looking Regan. Tears well in her eyes and an immediate need to protect her takes over. Just as I try to round on her, she shoos me away and hugs Mila.

"That would be amazing. These idiots," Regan sneers as she jabs her thumb at us, "have kept me away from there. I have been worried about how things are going and making sure the damn store hasn't burned down. There's thousands of dollars worth of books in there, and I can't afford for them to go up in flames."

If I had known she needed something for the store, I would have made something work. Well, I guess that reiterates the fact that there is still a lot to learn about this female of ours.

"Don't worry, we will take good care of you," Wini smiles gently, patting Regan's shoulder as they unlatch from one another.

"We need to get going," Warden interrupts as he looks up from his phone. "Troops are getting ready to move-"

"No missions talk in these buildings," Mila points out, her eyebrow raised in irritation. "It creates a negative environment for the children who are trying to leave this place and get a fresh start."

"We need to get going because the eagle is landing on a fucking bomb." He tips his own brow at her in a challenge, and she narrows on him. "Better?"

"No," she sneers, waving a hand at him. "But you can say your goodbyes. We need to get working on the dinner rush, anyway." The girls give Regan a quick hug, even Irene who appears standoffish, before hustling back to the main building.

Taking her sweaty hand in mine, we slowly walk back to the rear of the club where the pathway back starts. She tries to drag her heels to slow us down more, but Ghost takes her other hand and forces her to move. The poor female looks like she wants to cry. I'm having none of that. Stopping in my tracks, I scoop her up in my arms bridal style before continuing my stride. Shocked, she doesn't say a word, though she holds on tighter to Ghost's hand, refusing to let go.

She doesn't have to worry about that. Whether she likes it or not, she is ours. Until death do us part.

Chapter Twenty-Five

REGAN

Saying goodbye has never been easy, especially when there is a shitty feeling in my gut about them leaving me. There is nothing I can do or say to make them stay, so I do my best to stave off the impending tears until after they leave. Becoming a blubbering mess was not in my bingo card this year. It also doesn't help that I seem to have fucking stockholm syndrome or some shit. The thought of them leaving me has my stomach in knots and my brain frazzled with potentials of what could happen while they are gone. Is this what anxiety feels like? I don't like this shit one bit.

Viper walks easily with me cradled to his chest, his massive body radiating heat like a furnace. Cozy and warm mixed with the odd rocking from the walk have me nearly lulling to sleep. It wouldn't hurt for my eyes to shut for a few moments.

"Little Pyro," a hand is patting my face gently. "We want to say our goodbyes." That has my eyes snapping open. Looking around, I realize I must have fallen asleep. To be honest, it was an emotionally draining afternoon. I did a whole lot of nothing, which means I'm exhausted from doing literally nothing.

"I don't want you to go," I whisper as I curl my fingers into Viper's grown out blond hair. He grunts, his head tilting down toward mine. "My gut is telling me that you shouldn't go." There's a peculiar look on his face, one that I can't quite decipher, but it's gone as quickly as it came.

"Everything is going to be fine. We will be back by the end of the week, the end of next at the latest." He forces a smile onto his lips, one that looks completely plastic. It irks me that he's not taking this seriously, though they have been doing this a lot longer than I knew the club existed. If he feels safe doing what he needs to do, then I will have to trust him and the others on that. Trust isn't my strong suit, I can admit that without fault, so ignoring the gut feeling doesn't bode well with my head. My fingers curl tighter into his hair, the other hand resting gently on his cheek as I tilt his back and we connect. He doesn't hesitate in returning the gesture, his heart pouring into the kiss as I do. Molding into one he takes what I'm willing to give, and I'm taking just as much from him. A low rumble draws from his chest as his own fingers find my covered thighs, squeezing the flesh between his large hands and pulling me closer.

We let the kiss guide us. Heat sears hotter between the two of us as he slowly crawls over my body, my legs opening to give him space between them. Settling between my thighs, he grounds his thick, jean covered cock against my covered pussy. Hips snapping on me, there's a lot of friction but it's too inconsistent.

"More," I pant, moving my hands away from their current locations to grip the hem of his shirt. He pulls away, and for a second I think he's going to put a stop to this. Whatever look is on my face must be his last straw as he rips it over his head and connects his lips back to mine. In the back of my mind, I know that I'm trying to avoid the inevitable. Yet, if I can just get a few more minutes with him, maybe this feeling of helplessness will dissipate.

"Fuck, Regan," he growls, his accent getting stronger the more aroused he gets. "I can feel the heat of your cunt through your leggings and my pants."

"It's warmer without anything in between," I breathe out as best I can while my heart hammers in my chest.

"Such a fucking cock tease," he growls, sucking my bottom lip between his teeth and biting down. Groaning, I rock upward into him in an attempt to get more.

"Please, Viper. I need it." I sound as desperate as I feel. Thankfully, he can take the not-so-subtle hint. Letting my lip go, he scoots back far enough to pop the button on his jeans and shimmy them down his ass. His rock hard cock bounces out and smacks his bare abs while my mouth waters.

"If you need it so bad, then get fucking naked." The command is simple, quick, and I am in no mood to disobey it. My leggings come off way too easily, the material softly peeling down my legs. Viper is too impatient, grabbing hold of the waist and throwing them across the room. He crawls back over me, his face between my thighs. No warning given before he dives in.

"Shit!" I shriek as he devours me.

"We don't have a lot of time, so I want to make this count." His warm breath fans over my wetness, his fingers pulling the lips apart and toying with my clit. "You're so fucking sweet. Come on my tongue so I can fuck you hard and fast." His lips engulf my swollen clit, vacuuming it into his mouth and swirling it more. The tightness builds quickly in my core, my legs shaking as I threaten to strangle him with them. He doesn't seem to care as his eyes roll up into his head, and the tight ball explodes.

Stars dance in my vision as he laps at me, my fingers white knuckle gripping his hair and the sheets to try and keep myself grounded through the fastest orgasm of my life. He doesn't wait for me to come down before he crawls over my body and thrusts in. My hands don't have anything to grab as I thrash around for purchase. Slapping onto his back, my nails dig in as he drives into me deeply.

"Fuck, you're the perfect pocket pussy," he growls into my ear, biting my lobe harshly. There is no pain associated with the bite, but the level of possession in the movement has me clenching on him hard with a shrill cry when he hits a sweet spot. Rearing back, he plunges back into me as his hips swivel, the head of his cock nudging a deep, forbidden part of me that only him and the three others have managed to find. His pubic area brushes my clit with each forward push, but it's not enough.

"More," I gasp as I feel my nails finally break skin. Eyes rolling back and a growl of approval, he slams into me with frantic movements before sitting back on his heels. His large thumb is shoved into my mouth, and with a growl of warning, I suck it like it's a miniature version of his cock.

"What a good fucking cum slut," he groans. His feral nosies mixed with the slapping of skin has me barreling toward the edge of bliss. Ripping his thumb free, he circles it quickly over my swollen clit like it might disappear. The burning ache suddenly slams home, my mind going dizzy as blinding pleasure rakes through my body. It's intoxicating, and I can hear when Viper follows suit as he roars his release, his hand suddenly latching on my throat as he pounds savagely into me. He doubles over, and I have no idea where I start and he ends. Together, we muddle into one being of sweat, arousal, and bloody impulse.

"You would look so good with my name carved into your chest," I breathe out as the filter in my brain glitches. He groans loudly, his breath burning hot against my ear before he rises above me again.

"That sounds like a perfect gift for when we return." Reality slams back far sooner than I would like. Hoisting himself off of me and on his feet, he shimmy's his jeans back in place after stuffing himself away. "Now you have something to look forward to when we get back, okay?" I nod, my voice failing me as emotions run wild. My brain is still fuzzy from two intense orgasms, tingles lingering in my body from the loss of feeling throughout.

Gathering myself, I go to speak, but am interrupted by a knock. A few seconds go by as Viper and I stare at one another, neither one of us saying anything in fear of losing this. Finally, the door opens to reveal Maverick. With the subtlety of a true lady, I rush to pull the blankets over my naked half and to not reveal that I have his cum mixed with mine dripping onto the bed. No clue who even owns this bed, but as we can tell, I don't really care.

"We need to go," he emphasizes as he looks us over. Viper simply smirks at Maverick then grabs his shirt, hoisting it back over himself. Viper does one last glance over my body before walking out the door. Maverick comes over, leaning over the bed and gives me a quick but chaste kiss. "This mission isn't too far away and isn't supposed to be too dangerous, if that makes you feel any better."

With a look of incredulousness, I level him. "No, it doesn't." He laughs at me, shaking his head and standing.

"Remember, we are trained to do this shit. Just hang tight here and help the girls out, we will be back before you know it." With that, he turns on his heel and heads out of the door. For some reason, there's a sinking pit in my stomach. I wait several minutes, maybe even an hour, for Ghost and Warden to come to me, but they don't. My heart aches from their distance. Like Maverick said, they are trained professionals. They aren't used to having someone to say goodbye to and kiss on their way to work. It will take time for them to acknowledge that. Even with that knowledge it doesn't make the dark void in my chest any less painful.

Chapter Twenty-Six

Maverick

My grip on the throttle is loose as we ride south. The skull mask over my face keeps the breeze from suffocating me yet doesn't stop the wind from seeping into the fibers. It's freeing. Being part of the club hasn't always been easy, but times like these when we are on the open road aren't so bad. The cloud of impending doom that lays over the group isn't the best, but I digress.

Highway signs pass in a blur, and before we know it, we are taking turns toward our home base for the next week or two. A warehouse on the outskirts of town, dingy and malnourished from years of neglect. Slowly pulling into the gravel driveway, we all kick our stands down and stare for a minute. This makes me a little more appreciative of our clubhouse. It may not be the best accommodation, but it's what we could get on little notice. Heaving myself off the bike, my boots crunch the gravel as I walk toward the entrance. Each step causes little vibrations to shock through my legs, which is a usual aftermath of riding for so long. No other bikes or vehicles besides ours are here, and the description of the base is the same from what Shark indicated.

"Home sweet home," I grumble as I open the door. Mouth dropping, I'm actually surprised to see the inside isn't awful. There's a full bar in the corner, several booths scattered around the main area, and a large metal stairway leading to what I assume are the sleeping quarters. It looks almost like the inside of a prison with the set up, minus the bar. The rest of the guys shove past me, clambering into the area and settling with ease.

Looking around as everyone makes themselves at home, I can't help but still feel the emptiness of Regan. Somehow, over the course of a week, she's managed to chip her way into my dead, beating heart. Warden comes behind me before the door can slam in his face and falls on one of the other bunks. "Shit, I don't want to do this." Brows furrowing, I tilt my head toward him. Never have I heard him say he doesn't want to complete a mission. Usually, he's one of the go forth and conquer types.

"What's going on?" My question seems to fall on deaf ears when he doesn't answer for a while. His eyes remain unseeing at the ceiling above him, an emptiness I just now realize has been gone for the last week, because of her. Our fiery demon girl must have gotten us all under her thumb.

"Regan told Viper that something wasn't right. Ghost had that feeling the second we reviewed this case. I brushed Regan off because she's not used to the high life we have to live, but Ghost?" His sigh is heavy, the expansion of his chest deflating as he exhales longly. "His gut is never wrong." His head turns to look at me, and his eyes bore into mine.

"This is just another mission," I emphasize. Sitting up to look at him, I level him with my gaze. "We raid tomorrow, we leave the next." It's not an explanation, I know that. It's a shit cover for the fact that I'm feeling as uneasy as they are. There's no room in this equation for me to also be concerned. No hard evidence has been presented to the team that would say this mission has posed a higher threat than usual. Obviously we go in understanding that things are not going to be easy. For fucks sake, we ruin trafficking rings at the source, not the auctions. It's a frenzy filled with gunfire and death, and no evidence found by multiple parties would indicate a higher rise of risk. Due to the unease of Ghost, Shark provides an additional twenty men on top of our ten, then asked our sister club if they could procure a few men. So, we have around sixty men, not including the vans, assisting in this raid.

Getting off the bed, I make my way back to the open corridor and watch as men flit around the space. "Church, now!" I boom over the railing. They scramble to their feet without hesitation, making their way to the room that has "Chapel" above it. Ghost comes up behind me and claps me on the back.

"We just need to have faith that shit will work out the way it needs to." He moves around me toward the staircase, laughing with the guys as they convene into the room. I wait a while for them to trickle in before going down there myself. It's quiet in the main area, the eerie feeling in my gut only amplifying more. Nodding at a couple of the young prospects, they slam the doors shut behind me as I enter. It's so silent you could hear a pin drop.

It's weird being the center of attention as I'm usually flanking Shark, but this time I get to lead it. An odd feeling, that's for sure.

"We give thanks to Stallions of Steel for providing a safe warehouse for us to stay while on this mission," I start and they all mutter out a quick 'thank you' into the air. "There are two different locations that we will be looking at. One on the lower east side and one on the south east. They are about a ten minute ride from one another. We ride fast, we ride hard, and we execute those who get in our way while completing the mission."

Their faces are all stoic, even a few of the female prospects who wanted to be part of the assignment. I remember when females were fighting us left and right in an effort to be a patch holder. They wanted to wear their colors. Shark's dad, StingRay, was admittedly sexist, yet he told them to earn it. Ever since then, female prospects earn their colors. Like another sexist prick that he is, Shark makes them work nearly twice as hard to earn their spot. He says it's to make sure they know what they want. There's nothing I can do to make him change his mind, so I do my best to make it easier on them when possible. Now, keep in mind I don't give them pity or empathy. They are joining a rag-tag group of idiots who throw themselves into the line of fire. We do it for a cause, which is what a lot of the females say is their main purpose.

Grabbing the small ziplock from my pocket, I open the top and shake it. "In an estimate, we have close to a thousand children in the two bases combined. In a moment, you will all pick a paper at random. The color you get will be your assignment to either the south or the east. Red on the left, blue on the right." They line up one by one and grab their color at random. Quickly rolling through the paper, everyone has their assignments before it's just me and my three guys standing here. "You have thirty-two hours before the awakening sunset. I suggest you get plenty of rest because the next few days are going to be grueling in preparation. Warden and I will be leading team Red. Viper and Ghost will be leading team Blue. Jones and Hawk are going to stay here while we go into the buildings. Jones is red, Hawk is blue. If anything goes haywire, they know to abort the mission and work to get as many people out via a teleconference line as possible. Remember, we do not leave anyone behind, however if one of the team leads is down, you keep going." A few looks of shock ripple across the room, but the guys and I remain silent.

"Communication will be extremely limited, so speak now or forever hold your peace," Viper announces, his eyes searing into each person as he holds their gaze.

Met with silence, I wave my hand for them to disperse. As they haul ass out of the chapel, I stand here with my three closest allies and wait for them to fully vacate.

"You're as prepared as you can get, don't stress yourself out over unnecessary shit." Warden glances at me from the side but his focus remains toward the doors. "Prospects are getting paired with patches by Jones right now, so we don't have to worry about that." I nod, pleased with my right hand guy.

"You are responsible for one another, but if for some reason it's not safe for you to extract the other, you move on," I inform them as quietly as possible. "If one of us goes down, assess quickly. If it puts your life at risk, keep moving."

"How morbid," Ghost mumbles under his breath, his sideways glance burning a hole in my head. "I won't leave Viper behind, I will tell you that much." Knowing I can't convince him otherwise, I don't try to.

The doubt in my stomach is absolutely stemming from Ghost and Regan's paranoia, but I can't hold onto that right now. They continue to stand there, chatting amongst one another as I walk out. My head is far too clouded with noise for me to focus on anything around me. Taking the stairs two at a time, I can barely hold the fake ass smile on my face that falls the second I'm in the safety of the room. I don't bother to take anything off. Planting face first into the mattress isn't the greatest idea but it takes a few easy breaths before I'm out like a light with a feeling of dread settling inside of me.

Chapter Twenty-Seven

Ghost

Prepping in the Chapel is no joke. Several of the guys are smearing black paint around their eyes to shadow themselves further under their masks. Each one of us has a different variation of skull mask, but there's no mistaking who is who. Covered head to toe in black-out gear, we are ready to creep through the night without hesitation.

"There's no tomorrow without today, so we will fight!" I shout, raising my fist into the air as they chant 'fight, fight, fight'. Each raid gets us closer and closer to the main objective, kill off the Mountain Range Circuit altogether.

Riding to the area is a breeze as the baffles work like a charm while we silently pull into our lot. Bright flood lights illuminate the compound as their men walk the perimeter with weapons strapped at their sides. Halting our steps, we analyze their patterns, which matches what Globe told us previously. Their backs are uncovered, and it's only two of the same people. Viper stands next to me, scoping out air control for any signs of sniper or additional manpower we can't see. With a swift shake of his head, we are confirmed.

Placements are set, three members on the roofs acting as snipers flash their red lasers. Myself and the split team take the front while Viper and the other team take the rear. We spent a good portion of the morning analyzing the best raid areas, determining where the windows, exits, and other potential tunnels are positioned in the compound. Security footage was reviewed and confirmed. Now all that's left is for us to take immediate action. There's no telling when the other compound is raided or how that will go due to lack of communication, I can only hope they make it in and out successfully.

The two men round their corners and we move. Silently, we hustle toward the building with our guns poised. Each person scopes as we move to ensure we aren't blindsided. Grabbing the front of the door, I rip it out and a blaring alarm immediately sounds. "Go!" I shout, and they flood past me. Gun fire mixed with screaming reverberates along the metal walls, men in black running toward us angrily to prevent us from completing our mission.

Loose pipes are exposed in the ceiling as we go, some of them hissing from their screws as they build pressure. They go down easily, far easier than I would have thought. To these people, the children are considered high price cargo, so why aren't they doing more to prevent intrusions?

Questions race through my brain as I meet Viper and his team in the middle. There are several doors with staircases leading to the main medical area of the compound. Leaving them to ward off any incoming bullshit, Viper's team moves down the stairs and into the compound. There are several long doors that follow the corridor, all of them shut tightly with a padlock on the outside. One by one, we smash the locks on the doors and swing them open. A few of them are empty, the silence of the underground followed by the occasional gun shot. After ten doors, we realize there may not actually be anyone down here, but we don't stop. We check all thirty doors and come up empty handed.

"There were three other areas, we need to check those," I call out, motioning for Viper to take the lead again as I follow behind. We bump knuckles as he passes me, the longing in his eyes barely displaying through the thick mask he wears. Once the last runner is out, boots pound on the ground loudly. Our team wears blue on their arms to signify that they are one of us. There is no going back after getting shot, so it's better to be safe than sorry. I break away from Viper's team to check on mine. Several of the men are going hand to hand with the uncolored enemy. Rolling my eyes, I send a bullet through them and motion for them to hurry up. Kalli raises her gun toward me while pulling the trigger. I'm about to lose my shit on her when I hear a *thud* behind me. His head is blown, quite profusely, across the walls around me, the shocked expression on his face still plastered.

Barking at them to come on, boots hit metal loudly. We had the element of surprise, yet they are starting to surprise us. The sickening feeling in my stomach amplifies ten-fold as Viper meets us at the third corridor. "Nothing," he confirms. Growling loudly, I order Viper's team to take the fourth wing while we check the third. They had to have known we were coming. It would explain the blatant lack of manpower and skill, yet thankfully, I'm proven wrong.

"We got one!" Someone bellows out as they hold a child in their arms. They can't be more than twelve, their wide eyes scanning us with terror on their features. There's no time to comfort any of the children, so with a harsh jerk of my head, two of them march out with several more in tow. None of them are super young, and thankfully they don't look to be in bad shape. A little dirty, sure, but there doesn't appear to be obvious signs of starvation. We will let the women at the agencies look into them, though.

We work through all thirty doors, each room easily holding four kids that we manage to extract slowly and effectively. None of them put up a fight as we take them to the vans. I grab a toddler who puts her little head on my shoulder, and I swear I fall in love.

Odd time to think about having children, but the thought has my stomach turning with the same weird unease. Children of my own are out of the question, but I love being the cool uncle. The way I am with a lot of the kids who come out of these camps, I'm just the fun uncle who teaches them how to put a bullet in their enemies eyes.

Viper meets us at the top of the stairs with his own team carrying two at a time. Even through the mask, I can see his smile plastered on his face at the small victory. After they get back to the club, they have a lot of healing to do, but this is just the first step to doing that.

They get situated in the vans where there are a few nurses who are ol' ladies of the club helping them to get looked over while we work on clearing out the building. Another flood of guys in all black come pouring from the doors from the outside, and it's complete blood shed.

Sending off shot after shot, I end up running out of bullets and force Viper to cover me. He takes his own pace as I fight to get my mag out of the gun, but it's jammed. Reaching over to one of the other guys, I yank them toward me and grab their weapon. They don't argue with me as I aim it at the exposed pipes and fire off a round. Hissing echoes in the area as people shriek in pain. The steam is boiling hot as the heat radiates over to us. I don't know who it hit, but I can't focus on that right now. Giving back the gun, we manage to slowly push our way back outside while the men scream in agony on the inside from the steam boiling them alive. The area appeared contained, so I am very appreciative of that.

Hesitance grips me, but Viper and I complete one final sweep that shows they were definitely in the middle of clearing out of this compound. Movement to my right has me halting in my tracks, stopping Viper from going anywhere else.

"Gentleman, I think you have some things of mine that I would like returned." A man in a black suit steps over one of his dead foot-men, kicking the guy's limp hand as if he is disgusting. "I believe I can let this little....stunt go if you simply put my property back where you found it, hmm?" Viper's gun whips in front of him, but I halt him as fast as possible. The man's thumb is depressed into a button, one where I can see the outline is red.

"Why would we do that?" I ask as I decide there's more information to be had. If my training is correct, that's a decompression bomb, which means if he lets go of that button, we are fucked.

"You took my things, and I don't like when people steal from me." He must realize where my gaze is tracking him because his eyes light up immediately as he brings the hand holding the button up towards me. "Oh, this silly thing? It's nothing. It's just a button to make the place where your friends raided go ca-boom." He uses his other hand to mimic an explosion with a wicked smirk on his face. He looks oddly familiar, his features strong but soft, the jagged scar along the edge of his eyes...

Holy shit. It's Kastilof's right hand man. They share the same scar, only Getilad doesn't have the signature track marks like Kastilof does from where the stitches scarred.

"Alright," I affirm, my hands flying up to surrender. My brain can't grasp the situation yet my response mode is flying like words on a coded computer. "We have to page the others to bring them back in." There's no way for me to kill him and not have the alleged bomb go off. If Getilad is here, then Kastilof has to be at the other compound with Mav and Warden. He motions at us to get on with it while Viper looks at me like I have lost my fucking mind. Honestly, that's exactly what it feels like. Before I can blink, one of the others walks in silently and aims for his hand. Doing my best to not blow their cover while simultaneously telling them not too, it's too late.

Bullet hits skin and the button goes flying. Seconds later, the compound shakes as the echo of an explosion reverberates around us.

Chapter Twenty-Eight

Maverick

Kicking the door down is just as satisfying after the hundredth time, especially when you're immediately met with gun fire with the aim to kill you. Adrenaline spears into my system as we take off down the hallways. Metal grates cover the ground and we can see the main areas below that are devoid of anyone. Gripping my gun tightly, I branch off toward a staircase to the side of the main hallway and go down. Warden takes the other side to move efficiently, not wanting to waste any time standing around for them to attack us. The two individuals flanking my sides pop off shots as new attackers pop up in front of us while the rest of the group takes out intruders who attempt to attack from other angles.

"Left!" I bellow toward group B. They take off toward the left, nailing assailants immediately without fail. My team is strong, several of them having high rankings in precision when they were tested before being patched. It all works out as we race down the corridor and start scanning the location. We stop in a big, empty room that has several of the doors pried open. There are papers misplaced around the room scattered on the floors, needles dropped with the caps not on them. It's devoid of anything useful which tells me that they left in a hurry. Something must have tipped them off to our arrival, and I don't like that.

"Here!" Izzy calls from her location. There's a small child curled under one of the tables and shaking like a leaf. She scoops the kid up in her arms and hustles out of the room with three others flanking her, exactly like protocol indicated. We scan the room thoroughly, check through all the open rooms and make sure there aren't any vents unshed. Kid must have escaped during the rush and was able to hide. Resilience. We can work with that.

Taking the team back to the main area, we march back up the stairs to go down the other hallways. The blueprint in my brain is fuzzy, picture memory is not my strong suit, but if I can meet up with Warden, he can direct me where the next cell area is. Thankfully, they round the corner with a few of their own in their arms, rushing them outside toward the medical vans that wait. A few men went with them for coverage and several additional men stationed outside of the vans for safety. We can't keep them here for too long due to the risk, so there's a high level of efficiency that is required. Glancing at my watch, I realize there's only five minutes remaining before the vans take off. Once they are gone, we have to figure it out ourselves.

"Watch out!" One of the guys calls, and I immediately duck. A bullet whizzes past my head from an unknown source, another one following quickly behind it. It grazes the tip of my ear as I move out of the way. The guy behind me grunts in agony as he falls, and I do my best to move him out of the line of continued fire.

Men scatter away from the flying bullets and disperse down the other hallways. At least they appear to be following through on their missions and not waiting on me. Reaching up to grab my ear, I can feel the blood oozing down my face quickly. The hand that reaches in front of me is my own, yet the angry red blood that coats my skin seems to switch off another part of my brain that I can't quite understand.

After a few moments, I realize I'm by myself. I can hear crying in the distance as I run down the long bankway, searching for the asshole who tried to kill me. Warden and the team are handling everything else. A feeling in my stomach tells me that I know exactly what this is.

"Kastilof!" I bellow down the hallway, my voice reverberating off the walls back to my ears. "You want to kill me? Here I am!" Another bullet flies past me, and I turn on my heel, sending a few of my own. They don't hit anything except concrete, bouncing onto the floor from lack of penetration. Running in a zig-zag style pattern, more bullets whiz around me as I finally manage to gain coverage by turning a corner.

"Come on, Maverick, give me what I want and you can walk free," the deep voice bellows out. It sounds steady, almost like he wasn't running after me. "I need my property returned before the end of the night."

"They aren't your property," I spit as I peek around the corner and fire blindly in the direction his voice is echoing from. I don't wait to see if anything lands before pulling back around the corner. A shallow grunt is my confirmation that I made contact, I just don't know the level or impact of it.

"I beg to differ," he scoffs, his voice getting closer and closer but there's an angry edge to it now. "I got them fair and square. They are *mine!*" He turns the corner, his gun pointed directly at my head as I hold mine the same.

We both pull the trigger at the same time, yet neither one of us hits our targets as the ground shakes around us. His angry expression turns cruel yet happy.

"Your friend must have really pissed him off." I don't let him keep talking as I pull the trigger several times. Spraying his body with bullets doesn't seem to do anything as he remains standing with a wicked smile on his face. "You thought you had me?" His laugh is chilling, one that would haunt your nightmares as a child. My clip goes empty as the last of the bullets fly toward Kastilof's head. None of them land as he moves too fast. Real fear creeps up my throat as he keeps his gun trained on me, his features calm and cool.

Before I can talk, the ground shakes again, the sound of distant shouts the only thing keeping me grounded. Finally, with the sound of the pipes above us rattling, I speak. "It was you!" Thinking back to when Regan had that awful message in front of her door. He must know exactly what I'm talking about as he laughs louder.

"You liked my little treat, yes? It's awful knowing someone had to die for the cause, but money is money. When I realized you had someone to die for, it was the perfect opportunity. The only downside was when you all showed up. There wasn't nearly enough man-power to kill you all, but she would have made us a lot of money, too. I heard she's marked as yours now?"

We have a mole in our organization because there aren't many who knew that Regan was ours. Even less know of the marking on her back. How does he already know all of this? Has he been watching us as much as we have been watching him?

Rage I have never felt before rips through me as I roar, charging toward him. He raises his gun again, which I didn't realize had dropped, before sending off a warning shot near me.

"Let's not be dramatic, hmm? We live, we die, that's how it goes. I suppose you should be happy that you all got your heads out of your asses at the right time. She is quite the grumbler." He tilts his head back and forth at me, the gun dropping back down when he realizes I won't advance on him. There's no way I can get one up on him. "I'm itching for a fight, little man. Getilad never wants to fight with me, so if you win, you leave. If I win, you die and your girl becomes my property. Simple." He doesn't get to finish as I charge him, my fist slamming into his face with a loud grunt. He barely rocks back on his heels before he's throwing punches of his own. Cracks of bones in our faces echo as each deadly blow lands with harsh impact, my eyes tainted red from the split brow he managed to steal.

Blow after blow, we meet one another with level footing. Swinging on him doesn't do much besides make him hit harder, and I follow suit. There's no upper hand here, and with each passing second, the fire in my body is burning out. His stamina is better than mine as his jabs land harder and faster. I can't focus, the air in my chest is far too tight for the ability to breath. Bringing my hands in front of my face, I do my best to block his hits as he lands them. With a wicked cackle, he stands.

Admitting defeat is never something I thought I would do, but Kastilof has been in the business far longer than any of us combined, and I don't have backup. I told them yesterday that if someone went down, then that's on them. I guess this one is definitely on me.

"Sleep well, little girl," he sings as the floor below my bleeding body shakes. I can't see much as my eyes swell shut, but the pain radiating my body is enough for my brain to shut off as the fatal shot echoes through me.

Chapter Twenty-Nine

Regan

"We got the call!" Wini shrieks as she bounds toward the main room.. Just as she comes running in, the rumble of motorcycles coming toward the agency has everyone jumping into action. Well, everyone except for me. "Two major injuries, one deceased, several minor needs and the rest are in the clear." My stomach drops when I hear that someone died. The void that's been sitting inside of me is ripping me apart thinking it's one of my men. I even warned them not to go...

Irene rounds the corner, tossing medical bags at several people. My arms reach out to catch the bag that comes flying toward me as there are orders barked left and right. The glitch in my brain threatens to take over before Mila grabs my elbow and yanks me behind her. She doesn't say a word as we run outside where several vans pull through the rows of bikes.

Children come pouring out of the vans looking dirty and scared, but none of them appear to be skin and bones. So, at least there's one positive to this awful ordeal. Moving to go assist, Mila grabs my arm and shakes her head. Brows furrow deeply at her as she points to another van hoisting a covered body from the inside. A gurney suddenly wheels closer as they drop the bagged body onto it. The size is definitely adult, and my heart sinks when I look in the crowd of men and can't spot any of *my* men.

I can't go on pretending that they aren't mine. They've been gone for far too long, and every day they have been on my mind. Going to sleep was near impossible without them here. I didn't know if they were safe, didn't know what they were doing, didn't know if any of them had fallen...

Seeing the bag wrapped tightly around the individual doesn't do my aching heart any good. None of my men are in sight, and I don't see any of their bikes either. The loud rumbling of motorcycles still trickling into the lot keeps my hopes up slightly. I'm pulled in another direction as two seriously injured guys come toward us on gurney's, their eyes closed as an attached IV drips what I can only assume is medicine or saline into their veins. My heart beats a little faster when neither one of them look familiar, but I drift back to look at the covered body that's been pushed to the wayside. No one appears concerned as they work around him, and all of the emotions of the last few days bubble inside of my chest. Threatening to tear out of the group toward the body nearly overtakes me when Viper slinks around the corner with an ice pack on his shoulder. His deep gray eyes clash with mine, and I toss the bag to Mila then take off. Ghost rounds next to him which makes my heart sing with happiness that two of the four are here.

The moment I slam into Viper, the pent up emotions from the last few days come rippling in full force. With a small *crack*, the ice pack lands on the ground as both of his arms wrap around me tightly. Another body comes from behind me, dragging both Viper and I in. Warmth radiates from in front and behind me, and the contentment I feel temporarily gives my aching chest some reprieve. Pain behind my eyes has no comparison to the one inside of my chest as my two other guys aren't in view.

Just as I go to ask where they are, Mila calls over to them for help. There's a big dude who fainted on the concrete, his head cracked open from the fall. Ghost steps away first but not before placing a gentle kiss on my cheek. Viper taps my butt and my legs drop sadly. He meets my gaze with a depth of emotion I don't remember ever seeing from him.

I love you.

Mila shouts over again for help, and I let go of him reluctantly. Ghost is hauling the guy in his arms as if he weighs nothing, Viper follows behind his best friend as they chat about the next steps with Mila. Looking around at everyone, they all seem to have a job. Maverick said I would fit in with them easily, Haze said I would enjoy being in the library, but I haven't even had a chance to do any of that. We have been preparing for the next round of kids to come through, and I don't know if my heart can take the constant pain that it feels for these poor babies. Irene is chatting with a group of the young kids who appear to be eating it up. None of them seem malnourished, I don't see any bruises on them or any issues with them externally, but that doesn't mean anything. I don't have marks or bruises on my body, but the mental barrier that

I have would be an emotional tsunami for someone who hasn't experienced it.

The thought of Maverick has my entire being lighting up again, then I spot Warden kneeling by a few of the kids next to Irene. Her hand is on his shoulder and the way he smiles up at her...it's almost intimate. Though when he looks at me, the smile turns brighter as he excuses himself. Irene follows his gaze, and she definitely looks sad. No, I have to be seeing things.

Not able to think about it right now, he scoops me up with his arm banding around my back and his lips landing on mine with fire. I'm swept immediately by the kiss, the embers of fire in my stomach pop and light with each pass of his tongue. "I fucking missed you," he mumbles against my lips, and I couldn't have asked for a better man.

"I missed you," I whisper, pulling back and grabbing his face with my hands. His cheeks squish slightly in my grip, but that's when I notice the deep colored bruise on his eye and the busted lip. "You are all banged up." He smiles sadly before leaning down to capture my lips with his. Pouring his heart into the embrace, there's another feeling building up inside of me from him...

I love you.

"I have to finish writing up the report for Mav, but I will see you soon?" He asks as if I won't be here. Nodding, I can't get the words out of my throat to ask about Maverick. He's the only one I haven't been able to see. I feel like a teenager for the anxiety from not seeing my boyfriend during the passing period. Not being able to see him really has me questioning what is going on and the fact that no one seems concerned or even upset that he's not here. After a few seconds of stewing in my own irritation, I tap one of the guys' shoulders. He turns, lifting a brow at me in question.

"Where is Maverick?" The question is strong, demanding and definitely a lot more secure than what I feel. He doesn't immediately respond, instead looking up and around us for a few seconds before looking back at me.

"I think it's best if one of the guys talk to you." He turns around and walks away as I stare, gaping at him. The unease I feel doubles. I would think that either Viper, Ghost, or Warden would have told me if something happened to Maverick, but what if they are in mourning? The body on the side of the landing taunts me as I stare at it. It's slightly see-through, and I don't see any tattoos on the person through the bag. Maverick doesn't have any tattoos.

Another guy passes me, and I grip his sleeve, stopping him in his tracks. "Maverick, where is he?" The barked question has this dude's eyes widening in shock. Whatever he sees behind me has his scurrying away, and I catch Viper giving him the death glare. Wini comes up to me, grabbing me by the elbow and dragging me inside. Once we are out of ear shot, she turns on me with a perturbed look on her face.

"What's going on? You have been absolutely zero help, which is fine because we don't really need it, but the dude ran away with his tail tucked between his thighs," a slight smirk makes its way onto her lips as she talks, then she schools her features and narrows her gaze. "Spill."

Days worth of disquietude has me reeling, so when she demands it, she gets everything she asks for and more.

"Maverick hasn't shown up around here and no one is telling me anything. There's a dead guy off to the side that everyone seems to be ignoring and I don't get why. If he is one of our fallen, we are not treating him or her with the level of respect that they deserve. Viper and Ghost were so quick with their welcome because they have to be working on other stuff, but there's a level of discomfort in my chest that I can't seem to shake because no one is talking to me. Then, Warden brushed me off like I'm a nuisance after seeing me for a few short seconds, but at the same time he looked at me like I'm his entire world. My heart is telling me that I love them all, but my head is telling me that they are so much better off without me. Maverick is nowhere to be found, and that seems to be my driving force of anxiety right now. I know they don't like to talk about their missions and some of the shit they see is better off in the hands of you or Mila, but I can't help this slight niggling feeling in my chest that won't go away." Out of breath, Wini stands there with a soft expression. She doesn't appear to be judging me, but there is a recognizable emotion on her face. "Please don't pity me right now, I don't think I can handle it."

"I don't pity you," she scoffs, waving a single hand in the air. "I could tell from day one that those men are in love with you. There is a lot to unpack here, so I will make it quick, but it may be a good idea for you to stop by my office at some point for us to have a chat about this anxiety you're feeling."

"Whatever," I mumble knowing damn well that she's going to psychoanalyze me. Which is fine, but like, I don't want anything to do with that. I have trauma, whoopty-doo.

She holds up five fingers and starts ticking them off. "One, they are so in love with you that it's almost sickening. I hope to have at least one guy who makes me feel like I walk on the red carpet everyday, let alone four. Two, the guy in the body bag is the right hand man, Getiland. He is the main hit-man that works operations to bring the innocent ones into their horrible mess. We never bring back the men of the fallen to the exchange, they get taken to the main clubhouse where a few of the prospects prepare them for services. Three, they do have a lot to do and I'm glad you are able to notice inside of yourself that they aren't brushing you off. When they aren't running around like crazy and getting themselves together, they will give you the necessary greeting. A lot of girls who come into the club feel brushed off the first couple of missions, but those men can't stop their duties once they come back. Reports need to be completed, interrogations need to be done if they capture someone, integration for the children has to take place, and so much more. They can't stop once they get back, but I can see how hurtful it is to feel brushed off. It is on them for not explaining it before they left, so I would recommend telling them how you feel when you can all get a moment of peace."

A lot of information is being spewed at me, but I deflate entirely knowing that Maverick isn't the one laying in that body bag. Literally hate when people talk logic to me, yet I can't help feeling grateful for her right now. There is a lot going on, a lot of moving parts that I don't know anything about, so it definitely was a relief to know that they aren't brushing me off. Again, these juvenile feelings rear their ugly heads.

"Four," she starts again, bringing my attention back to her. "I think you have a lot of your own unhealed trauma. With the way you reacted, I would say there may be some level of abandonment that you feel as well as a need for constant reassurance. That's just from what I have noticed, though. I would go as far as to say that I'm seeing some insecure attachment issues that I think we could work through together. This will be between you and me, but there's a need for you to be comfortable in your skin. From the outside, it's pretty clear that you aren't even remotely feeling safe inside your own body."

It would be rude to punch her right now, huh? From one little rant, she is able to pin-point every one of my fatal flaws. Tears well up behind my eyes, and I angrily rub at them, willing them to go away. I refuse to get emotional over this shit.

"That doesn't explain why I fear so much that Maverick isn't here," I hiss sadly, and she just smiles at me.

"Shit, I could have told you that before," she shrugs as she grabs another clipboard from behind the desk. "They are in love with you as much as you are in love with them, obviously."

Chapter Thirty

Warden

Filling out paperwork has never been so grueling from what I can remember. Typing out every detail is near impossible, so as I work my way through my report, I have to go back ten spaces when I recall it in more intimate details of the encounter. After I walked away from Regan, I felt a sense of unease. Questions were silently spoken in her eyes, but there wasn't any time for me to decipher what they were. There was a mixture of heartache and confusion without any explanation. I saw Ghost and Viper hug her before I could get to her, and that was perfectly okay with me. She was in good hands for the time being while I got caught up with the children Irene was talking to.

    The guys don't go into the agencies, so when we do our meetings with the children and the pass-offs to the agency staff, we do it outside. Kneeling in front of them and chatting about their next steps in life is usually my favorite part. Yet, when I felt her burning stare in my head, looking up into her eyes and seeing the excitement shining brightly...that is my new favorite part of coming home. The way she clung to me and wrapped her arms around me, I couldn't help going in for the kill. We kissed like we hadn't seen one another in a year, though it was only a few days. Words I have never spoken out loud laid at the tip of my tongue as we made out, and I did my best to pour them into her being as we reconnected.

"How's it coming along?" Ghost asks as he comes behind me. Shrugging, I do my best to focus, and fail, at paying attention to the report. He plops down on the chair next to me where Viper quickly follows suit, falling into Ghost's lap.

"Did something seem off with Regan?" Viper asks, his mouth stuffed with bread. Whipping my head toward him, I balk at him.

"Can you read my mind or some shit? I was thinking the same thing." Ghost and Viper exchange a look, both of them completely uneasy.

"She just seemed off, but I don't think it has to do with us. I assumed it was because everything was happening at once. I mean, with the shit that went down with Mav..." Ghost trails off, a saddened look on his features. "Fuck, I miss him already."

"When is the service?" I ask, swallowing down the lump in my throat. I can't get over the shit that went down, and the fact that we lost one of our brothers so early on. The weight of death is never fun, and especially when they are part of the club...agony washes over me for him. It could have been worse, I suppose. Death is inevitable.

"In two days, after the kids are settled down and everyone is notified of the passing." Viper's twang is deeper than usual, the emotion of losing our own hitting him hard. I think we are all in a shit situation right now, and there's nothing we can do about it. Like I said, we can't avoid death, so we have to mourn happily for those who have fallen. "I'm done with my report, and I'm exhausted. I'm going to get Regan and see if she wants to curl up on the couch with me for a nap." He pats Viper's ass with his hand, hauling himself to a stand before walking away. Viper plops himself back down on the chair and swivels in it quietly. I go back to my report, my brain unable to focus with the loss striking so fucking close to home.

Chapter Thirty-One
Regan

Ghost walks in through the double doors, not bothering to listen to Wini telling him to fuck off. He leans down, grabs me by the thighs, and hoists me over his shoulder like a sack of potatoes. Talk about a man with no chill, though he's getting absolutely zero complaint from me as he hauls me out of there like a caveman. With a shit-eating grin on her face, Wini uses the pointer finger on one hand and circles her thumb and pointer on the other to make a fucking motion. I just blow her a kiss. The missing piece in my chest still throbs harshly as I think of Maverick not being here, and it also doesn't help that no one is willing to tell me anything.

Silence encapsulates us as he walks us back to a room, I can only assume it's his and Vipers, before ever-so delicately body slamming me sideways onto a couch. *"Oomph!"* I huff as air puffs out of my lungs from the impact. His wicked smile stretches his plump lips, and my instinct takes over as I reach up, wrap my hands around his neck, and bring him down to me. His soft lips slant over mine as I widen my thighs, giving room for his large frame to fit. With a swivel of his hips, he slides himself to his knees bringing me to sit up and bend down just slightly.

Detaching himself from me is a chore, but when he does, the level of eye contact he gives me is an entire body experience. "I missed you so much," he whispers as his head leans against mine, his breath coming out hot against my face.

"You have no idea how much I missed you." He nods against me as if he knows exactly what I went through. Calloused hands land on my covered legs, and the roughness of his palms catch on the material as he skims my thighs. "Kiss me." Raising a single brow, his lip twitches mischievously as his hands taunt the waist of my leggings. His fingers curl into them, pulling down my body, and I lift my hips to help him take them off.

"I have plans to kiss those pretty lips," he teases but doesn't make eye contact, and it takes me a second to realize he means my pussy. The blush that creeps onto my cheeks has no business being there, but when he finally realizes that I went commando, his eyes deepen with unmistakable lust. "Is this all for me?" The question lingers in the air between us as he leans forward, shoves my upper body back, grabs under my knees, and yanks my ass nearly off the couch. I squeal softly at the swiftness, but when his tongue makes contact, my entire body jolts with need.

I nod and he brings his rough hands back up my legs, using his thumbs to part my lower lips. He stares at my pussy for several long seconds, much longer than I would anticipate as I start wiggling with discomfort. Eyes flicking up to meet mine, he grins widely before diving back between my thighs. Skilled movements meet my swollen clit as he swirls, sucks, and flicks his tongue over my sensitive bundle of nerves. One hand strays away from my pussy lip and trails toward my breast. Sliding under the cup of my bra, he takes my already taut nipple between his fingers and pinches.

"Oh," I sigh as my hands finally join the action. I grip his wrist to keep him exactly where he is and use the other hand to take a fist full of his dark hair. He growls against me as I tug at the root keeping him latched onto my clit. The vibration sends swirling pleasure through my entire being, my toes curl as he hauls my leg over his shoulder then slides two fingers into me unceremoniously. My back bows off the couch as he slams right against my favorite spot and pumps.

"Fuck, I can feel you swelling," he grunts against my clit as he brings me the most absolute pleasure. His finger works me from the inside out, my brain fraying with need for more, but with each drive of his hand, my pussy gets more vocal. "Squirt for me, pyro, soak my fucking face with your cunt."

"Ah!" I shriek as I'm shoved over the cliff. There's a weird urge building inside of me as liquid spills from my body. My eyes are open, but I can't see anything past the sheer-white bliss I feel right now. "That's my girl, look how soaked my face is," he glances up from between my legs with a smirk on his face. Legs quivering, body trembling, he doesn't let up as he coaxes me toward another ledge. "No, no," I beg as I attempt to shove his head away. Well, my brain attempts to shove him away but the tight hold I have on his hair keeps him wound tightly to my center as I build for another mind-blowing orgasm. Just as I reach the precipice, he pulls away. Again, I chant, "no, no, no," which he seems to find funny because he laughs evilly.

"When you come next, it will be on my cock." He undoes the button on his jeans which seems to let go of the pressure against his raging hard-on. Gripping the underside of my legs, he brings my ass off the edge of the couch and lines himself up. "I can't wait to stuff your pretty cunt full of my cum and watch you struggle to hold it in there. I want to see your pussy overflowing with my cum and just when you think it can't hold anymore, I will give you more." I swear there's an 'or else' on the underlying bite of his tone, but I don't want to make a threat out of it. Instead, I nod overly enthusiastically.

He grabs his thick shaft and rubs the dark head from my hole to my clit, smearing my juices over the length of me. Several more times he barely notches himself inside of me before pulling out and teasing me. Digging my fingers into his shirt, I yank him close to me, my patience snapping. "Put your fucking cock in me."

"Oh, that is very rude of you," he taunts as he pulls his hips away from me more. "You need to learn your manners before I can give you my cock." Rearing my legs back, I plant my feet on his chest and push. He doesn't see it coming as he tumbles onto his back, gasping in surprise. Lurching myself off the couch, I straddle his lap and impale myself onto him. The stretch is burning from the tight fit yet that's exactly how I love it. His fingers grab my hips immediately as he keeps me steady.

"I think you were very rude to deny me what I want," I taunt back as I rotate my hips. The head of his cock bumps the perfect spot inside of me, so I do it again. "How about if you want to come, you beg *me*?" Fire flashes in his eyes as he suddenly lets go of my hips, his tattooed torso stretching as he brings his hands behind his head.

With a tilt of his hips, he's pressing deeper inside of me. The smirk on his face has me guessing he knows exactly what he's doing. "Think you're a big girl, hmm?" I nod, rolling my hips over his again then tilting them up and off. "Show me."

Slamming down on top of him, his mouth drops open in an 'o'. I plant my feet next to his hips, using my glutes, thigh muscles and momentum to bounce on his hard length. With each drop, his muscles strain. An odd feeling overtakes me, and I pop off. He opens his mouth to question me, but I drop my hips over his mouth with the silent command. His brow quirks up before moving his hands to my thighs and latching onto my clit.

"Eat my fucking pussy like the good fucking boy I know you can be." Swirling my hips, I goad him into submission. Knowing him, I had to take it, not ask for it. "What do you think about calling Viper up here, hmm? Think he would take your ass while I fucked your face?" Eyes bright, he nods against my flesh. *Tsk*ing him, I reach over to where his pants are splayed and grab his phone. Angling it just right, I snap a photo of him getting partially suffocated between my thighs. A quick text to Viper and I'm tossing the phone away from us.

He feasts on me like a man starved, not letting my legs go as my hips start to go numb. I don't know how long I have sat here or how long ago I sent that text, but Viper comes crashing into the room with Warden trailing behind him. Then, a fourth body comes peeking around the corner, his arms crossed over his body.

"Maverick," I whisper.

Chapter Thirty-Two

Regan

I shove my way off Ghost as I bolt toward Maverick. He smirks at me like he knows I have been worried as fuck about him but wanted me to sweat it out. Obviously, I was orgasming it out because if I didn't, I would have done something stupid like go out to find him. Flinging myself onto him isn't the most graceful, but when he catches me, it's game over. My lips slam onto his as I fight for control over my emotions. He just smiles into the kiss as I use my heels to work his pants down his legs. When he hisses, I drop myself from his hold as much as he lets me.

Keeping me close to him, he just shakes his head. "I'm alright, just a bit banged up, that's all." His fingers brush sweaty stray hairs from my face as he takes in my disheveled appearance. "We can talk about what happened later. For now, I want to see you sit on your throne." Gently guiding me away from his body, he nudges me back toward Ghost. With a shy smirk, I kneel over Ghost's face with my back to the group, tilting my hips forward so they can get a good look at my pussy.

Collective groans echo through the room as I wiggle over Ghost's tongue. A hand bounces off my left ass cheek, then my right as the *smack* vibrates through me.

"Fuck, I want to fill that ass," Viper snarls as he comes in front of my face with his cock in his hand. Well, someone is eager to join the party. "Suck." My tongue falls from my mouth as I lick at the bulbous head of his cock like a lollipop. Viper looks down at me, then next to me where his other half is laying nearly suffocated by my pussy. At least he will die doing something he loves.

"Eat her pussy like it'll be your last meal." The order comes from behind me, but my focus isn't on the others. Right now, it's giving Viper's cock the attention it deserves. One hand latched in Ghost's hair, the other comes under Viper to cup his heavy balls, rolling them around in my palm. When I finally suck his cock down my throat, he jolts even further from the suction and me pulling on his sac.

"Show me what else you can do with that mouth." Viper lifts his leg onto the ottoman near him, exposing his whole lower half to me. Stretching as far as I can, I suck his heavy balls into my mouth and coat them with my saliva. Once I'm satisfied that he's on the brink, I let them drop out and spit on my fingers. He knows exactly where I'm going with this because he gives me a slight nod as I work my finger into his tight ring. Head falling back, he groans as I suck the head of his cock and prod his asshole.

Ghost must be watching because the sounds and vibrations against my clit have me barreling toward my orgasm much faster than I would like. Control is mine as I lift my hips off of him and he groans with irritation. I get off of him, kneeling in front of Viper and force him to join me by yanking his shirt. Thinking better of it, I grab the collar of it and tug. Ghost takes the cue and rips it over his head quickly before kneeling next to me with Viper's thick cock in our faces.

"I want Viper to fuck you in the ass," the words from my lips seem so natural that I'm not even shocked by them. If you would have asked me two weeks ago if I would say these things, I definitely would be called a stuck-up prude. Now? I want to watch them fuck while I get fucked off to the side. I want to enjoy their love for one another while lavishing in my own sex-style spa day. I want the guys to make love to me on a more primal, aggressive level...

Make love.

Are we really at that point yet? I mean, it's been less than two weeks and I have already fallen head over heels for them. That can't be natural...looking at their faces with the deep-set love they hold for one another with the reflection coming toward me, I can see it.

"What do you say, Ghost? Want my big cock in your tight ass?" His deep drawl has my pussy getting slicker with need. The two of them are hot individually but when they are together, it is a scalding hot burn. Ghost looks over at me for confirmation, and I do my best to show him that he doesn't have to if he isn't comfortable. Finally, he looks up at Viper and nods. Viper grabs Ghost's hair, jerks him to stand and moves their giant bodies to the bed. I stay kneeling on the floor, unsure what to do with myself before Maverick and Warden take up the space in front of me.

Cocks in hand, they both stroke themselves in my face. "I want to fuck your throat so bad," Warden hisses as his fist clenches tighter and pumps faster.

I'm so fast to reply, I don't think my brain even had the thought. "Do it." Maverick and Warden share a look I can't quite decipher, then Warden guides himself down my throat slowly, ensuring I'm prepped and open. Pulling out, he takes both fists, wraps them in the roots of my hair, and lets himself go. My eyes close on their own accord as he takes me the way he wants me, my nails digging into his thighs as I hold on for the ride, or in case I need him to let up. What seems like seconds after he starts, there's a probing at my lower half that has me clenching my body tightly.

"Relax, Little Pyro," Maverick's deep voice whispers into my ear, his teeth latching onto the lobe for a split second. He pulls it taut before letting it go, the cool sensation on my ear mixing with the heat from Warden roughly using my throat. Cold fingers probe my asshole as he invades on my most intimate area. "Your asshole is so tight, I'm tempted to rip through it." A hum of agreement falls from me ahead of my thought process that says tearing through my ass probably isn't the greatest idea.

"Could you imagine all the blood our girl would pour? She already makes lube from one hole, it would be her giving us more lube from her other." Warden knows exactly how to make bad ideas sound amazing, and right now, I'm pretty sure they could get me to jump off a bridge with the way I'm feeling. "Our masochist likes that idea, doesn't she?" Again, I can only nod with his cock shoved down my throat. He laughs tightly as I swirl his balls in my hand. The stretch at my rear brings me closer to the brink faster than I would have imagined, which he must notice because he pulls away quickly.

"No coming until you are told. You may have been able to walk all over Ghost, but when I tell you to do something, you will do it." Stern Maverick is a lot hotter than I remember. Him being alive is more than enough for me, so when Warden pulls out of my mouth, I turn sharply and attack Maverick. He laughs as we fall to the ground, a feral piece inside of me snapping as I drop onto his long, thick cock.

"I thought you were dead," I whisper as I move quickly over his lap. A thin piece of my sanity is hanging on by a thread as I portray the fear I carried all day. "You cannot leave me. Cannot leave *us*." Tears border my lash line, but I blink them away and channel my sadness into him. He can absorb my sadness and turn it into something more, and that's exactly what I want.

Warden trails his fingers over my spine, digging them into spots along my spine as I move over Maverick. "You're so fucking sexy when you show off that you're ours," Warden mutters darkly as he moves away completely. The flick of a lighter strikes the back of my mind causing me to freeze. Maverick's dirty brown eyes twinkle with humor, he knows that lighters are my sweet spot. I have been trying to break my habit of playing with them since I'm going to be working around vulnerable people, but that simple strike of the flint has me feeling like a druggie in relapse. A candle comes in front of my face, it's the shape of a rose. It's melting quickly, and I can't help but focus on the flame and the smell of the burning wicker. Drawn like a moth, I lean back instinctually as Warden drops a few droplets deliberately over my nipples. From my last time playing with wax, this isn't nearly as hot. The pain isn't the same biting kind I enjoy, but I'm not complaining.

More wax pours over me, several small drops landing on Maverick's chest as we are both painted red. My hips never stop moving, his cock hitting that beautiful spot inside of me as the heat draws me to a sizzling orgasm. Like burning embers, there needs to be something *more* to catch it on fire. After the candle is mostly gone, Warden disappears from sight as Maverick turns us ever so slightly, and Ghost and Viper come into view. Ghost is bent over the arm of the chair, Viper working his cock inside of his best friend. Watching them spurs me on even more, but I halt when the probing at my ass starts again. I watch as Warden takes a small blade and moves it toward where his hand is currently massaging my tight ring. "This is going to sting Little Pyro but we all know you love the pain." With a quick flick of his wrist, he knicks my asshole and quickly slices little cuts around it. "Look how beautifully you bleed for me. I can't wait to see that blood coating my dick as I fill you with my cum." He leans forward and begins to rub his thick cock head around my tight ring, collecting all the blood. "You ready Little Pyro because I am not going to be gentle."

Slamming my eyes tightly closed, the two men playing with me feel so far away as they reassure me. "Don't clench, it makes it worse." I just nod, and when the tip of his cock notches my ass, I can't help the moan that leaves me. Maverick reaches between us to brush my clit, and it takes my entire body to keep still.

"Your ass is like heaven, if one existed," Warden relishes behind me. I'm disgusted in the best possible way, their cocks rubbing together through me and connecting them in a way they never would have imagined. "Stay still for a second," he huffs while trying to catch his breath. The giggle that spews out of me isn't planned, and both guys groan.

"Is she clenching tightly onto you too?"

"Fuck yeah."

Finally, they start moving. Together they feel far too big, but when I shift slightly and tilt my hips, it's game over for me. Their cocks graze parts of me that I thought were a myth. Screaming with glee, I release the pent up energy. Both men make noises, but the heady feeling has taken me out of this fucking galaxy. I swear this is a form of intoxication. My entire body vibrates with need as they use my holes for their own personal pleasure. Each movement keeps my orgasm from going away, that or they are building another one before the first can even dissipate. Whatever it is, jolts of fire run through my nervous system as growls of ecstasy reverberate around us. Ghost is getting pounded into on the couch from behind, their noises being a key factor to the second or third orgasm that builds in my core.

Writhing over them, I can't stop the hissing pleas that release from me. "Don't stop, don't fucking stop, I'm going to fucking come!" Thankfully, they don't change their pace or stop, bringing me back over the brink of pure chaotic bliss. "Yes!" Liquid comes rushing out of me, the squelching sounds met with each thrust from the guys as stars build behind my eyes. This level of sex shouldn't be fucking realistic, but here I am, getting pounded into the next century.

Orgasm after orgasm, they wring me completely spent before they all come. Viper and Ghost stop mid-thrust to come over to me, pumping their rock-solid cocks in my face and dumping their load all over my face. My traitorous eyes refuse to open after several minutes, and I doze to their soft chattering with one another, the comfort of having all four of them back settling the unease in my chest.

"You look so beautiful covered in our cum. Watching it drip out of your holes is doing something to me." Maverick whispers into my ear as I feel him pushing the cum back into my pussy. "One day soon, this belly will swell with a child that is ours to love. I'll make sure of it."

I don't know about all that but I am game to practice. That is the last thought I have as I finally find the peace I needed to rest.

Chapter Thirty-Three

Ghost

"Fuck, you're so hot," I groan as Regan takes me to the back of her throat. What a way to wake up! She does some sort of growling, choking sounds because it vibrates along the ridges of my cock, sending the feeling directly to my balls. "Bring that pussy up here, I want a taste."

With a solid *pop*, she unlatches and quickly straddles my face. Arms winding around her thick thighs, I force her to put weight on me as I lick from her clit to her ass sliding my tongue past her tight ring.

"Yes," she sighs as she drags out the 's'. She leans down again, her mouth being filled with my big cock as I jut my hips upward. Gagging, she yanks herself off my cock and presses her hips further down onto me. I grin.

"Suffocate me, baby." She laughs as if I'm joking but keeps the weight there. "Fuck, I think one of the guys should come fill this pussy while I eat you out." Mav doesn't waste any time getting to his knees by my head, ogling her tight cunt as she spasms over me. Each lick and nibble of her clit makes her opening flutter. Rolling my eyes up toward Mav who kneels above me, his heavy sac dangles just above my head. He drags the blunt tip of his cock over her opening, gathering her juices and smearing them down his shaft. The sight has me bucking my hips into Regan more.

"Look at you sucking Ghost's fat cock so fucking well," Viper drawls. I can't see him from here, but I can hear that he's down by Regan's head. "I should have you wet my cock too, prep me to take Ghost's ass." The bed shakes with the force of her eager nod and anticipation drags up my chest as I work her clit faster. Her hips and legs tremble as I keep her latched to me, Mav still teasing her opening as she fucks my face.

"I love that idea," Mav says, a soft chuckle having me look up at him. "Maybe Warden should fuck her ass while I fuck her pussy. Then Viper can take your tight ass." Regan must also enjoy that idea because a drip of cum leaks down her and drops directly into my mouth. With an audible slurp, I devour her harder.

"Shit, I'm going to come," she garbles around my cock. Mav takes that as his cue to slide into her in one swift thrust. She surges forward to try to get away but fails as Mav's hands sit on the hinge of her hips and help me keep her latched down.

"You're going to come and you are going to take it," Mav growls as he rears back, slamming into her. I swear I feel the dip in her lower stomach as he takes her hard but slow. My knees are parted as a set of hands glides over my legs, rubbing soothingly across my heated flesh.

"What a way to wake up," Viper mutters, his fingers grazing over my cock as Regan takes me deep. I can't see what he's doing, but from the feel of it, he's scooping up her spit to-

"Oh fuck," I groan loudly. This is too stimulating and we are just getting started. With a loud pop, I'm suddenly speared open, the burn has me hissing against her clit.. There was no warm up, the way I like it, as Viper thrusts himself into me slowly.

The bed dips as Warden straddles above me and in front of Mav. That's a fucking image. Closing my eyes, I just let everything feel around me. Her gagging on Vipers dick has her entire body shoving backward onto Mav and Warden. They groan in unison above me as I rock to stay connected to her clit. A female shriek of agony washes over my body, my eyes slamming open to assess the danger. From what I can see, Warden is shoved completely inside of her, a trickle of blood running from her ass into her cunt where Mav is fully seated inside of her. Eyeing the blood droplet, my dick is suddenly wrapped back in her warm mouth as a sob rips up her throat. I can't see if she's only in pain, but when I suck her clit into my mouth and ramp up the speed, she begins rocking back slowly again.

Pressure builds in my lower abdomen as Viper starts inching his way into me. Regan's saliva is doing wonders as he shoves deeper and deeper, the tip of his cock massages against my prostate in a pulsing movement. A mix of a groan and a growl is pushed onto Regan's clit as I use my teeth to scrape the bundle of nerves.

"What a good listener our female is," Viper teases, the sound of flesh slapping flesh above me has me focusing away from the blood dripping. Tilting my head to the side, I see Mav eyeing up Warden's ass, his fingers tightly gripping the hinge of Regan's leg while his gaze goes between Regan's cunt and Warden's ass.

Mav must sense me eyeing him because he looks down at me, a deep red blush tinting his cheeks as he continues to move in rhythm with Warden.

"This ass is so ripe for me," Warden mutters, his voice low as he bends over Regan's back completely. From the way his voice was muffled, I would say his face is in her neck while Viper holds her hair out of the way. "Fuck, you bleed so good for me, Little Pyro." That has all of us groaning in agreement.

"I'm going to fill this fucking pussy with my cum, and you're going to fucking thank me for it," Mav calls, his hips slamming against hers and his stomach bumping Warden's ass. What I see next should surprise me, but it definitely doesn't. Mav raises a hand and sends his palm landing smack into Warden's ass, a bright red hand print present for all to see. Warden shouts with pleasure as I watch their balls draw up into their body.

Viper begins to move inside of me, his hand cupping my balls as Regan's hot mouth takes me to the back of her throat. Choking sounds hit my ears as her tight throat encapsulates my cock with each drop of her head. Eyes slamming shut, I will away the onslaught of the impending orgasm. Viper chuckles at something, and when he pulls on my balls, I'm a goner.

With a muffled cry, I suck her clit into my mouth and don't let go until the swollen bud starts pulsing. She doesn't come off my cock like I would expect her to, instead keeping me fully into her throat as my load covers her mouth. Viper's body slams into mine, his long cock rocking into me as he slowly brings me back to the edge of an orgasm. My cock doesn't deflate as I gear up for round two.

"That's right, come on my cock," Viper snarls as he pummels inside of me. Regan takes to sucking me even harder, her cheeks hollowing as she gags, chokes, and deep-throats my thick cock. "You will come with me, or I will make you start all over." Viper is fucking bossy when he gets to be the top, but I'm not complaining. Nodding, I tilt my hips as I start fucking her throat. She suddenly stops moving against me while I work myself down her throat, silently begging for Viper to hurry the fuck up because my balls tighten again and I'm on the verge.

"Her ass is too fucking tight," Warden snaps as he and Mav work in unison above me. More blood travels from her, but this time it's not from her ass. Her cunt is bleeding, and it's threatening to drop on my face. I'm fucking here for it. "Shit, shit, shit," he chants as he slams into her once before bellowing his release. Mav follows right behind him, his cock buried to the hilt as they remain still. The juices mix within her cunt, and I detach from her clit as she screams around my cock. I wait for the single droplets to fall on my tongue, my eyes closing in pure bliss.

Stretching, I roll over and wrap my arm around Regan. She snuggles deeper into my body, her perfect curves matching the hard ridges of my body.

"So, now that we are all sated, does anyone want to tell me how Mav came back from the dead?" I raise my brows, unsure what she's talking about. So, I ask.

"Little Pyro, we live by the rule that if one of us falls then we aren't to go back for them. There is a lot we need to talk about but the guys all need to be here for it," I say next to her, my mind buzzing with a lot of questions. "Do you want to talk about how you felt when we came back?"

"I couldn't see Maverick anywhere… He just was gone while I saw the three of you, then no one would tell me what was going on… Everyone just went on about life like he didn't matter. I was scolded for wanting answers. Even you guys seemed to brush me off. I know that I am new to this world but you didn't even prepare me for what to expect. You say you want me to be part of this yet you left me woefully unprepared for what to expect and what the expectations of my role here would be. Your crew was upset with my behavior like I should know better." Regan sniffles as I bring her in tighter. We fucked up by not doing aftercare with her, I know we were all exhausted but we have to do better. I fear that most of this is a let down from the high of a group session.. Treading lightly is the way to play it.

"Baby, he was perfectly fine," I mutter, kissing her head. "There is a lot that goes on when we come back from a mission. Mav usually handles the harder things of coming back, and he wasn't here. We were all processing the loss of one of our brothers in arms but we couldn't let those kids down by abandoning our duties. I am sorry that you felt pushed to the side and I agree we should have done more to prepare you for what to expect, not only from the mission but for what happens after. I promise once Mav is back, we will tell you everything.." She sits up slightly and looks around the room. Viper and I are the only two left.

"Warden and Mav had to go get some other shit done, but they promised they would be back to chat with you later. Remember we have responsibilities inside the club that can't be pushed off." The sadness in her eyes breaks my heart a little, and I want nothing more than to make it go away.

"I was so heart broken when I thought..." she shakes her head, cuddling into me further.

"You think that asshole is easy to get rid of?" I ask, causing a giggle to bubble out of her chest. She shakes her head, leaning up to look at me. Dipping my head, I meet her in the middle for a soft kiss.

Only, it definitely doesn't stay soft.

Epilogue

Maverick

"What do you have?" I ask, sitting next to Globe. He pushes his glasses up his nose as he looks over the screen.

"Kastilof is on the run again, but we are working to pin-point his location once more. He realized we were onto him previously, so that forced him back into hiding." Cursing under my breath, I lean my head into my hands. "He frequents several locations around the area, even big name casinos. Pretty sure Black Viper's MC spotted him yesterday at one of their local bars. We will find him."

"Maverick, here's that paperwork you asked for." Irene's tone is blank, irritation on her features as she walks into the tech room. Globe doesn't seem to pay her any attention, clicking away on his computer. "Kastilof is a slippery son of a bitch, huh?" That has him snapping up to look at her. The second he lays eyes on her, he's entranced. She's a pretty girl, just not for me. Glancing between the two, the tension is the air is practically crackling with lightning.

"Yeah, he definitely is, but we will catch him," I say cautiously. Both of them seem to snap out of their stupor, shaking their heads. She doesn't say another word as she turns on her heel, barely remembering to give me the damn report I asked for. Brushing off that weird interaction, I flip through her write-ups on the individuals that don't have relatives or anyone willing to come get them. We will work on integrating them into the club in the upcoming months.

"Who was that?" Globe asks as he still watches where she left.

"Irene? She works over at the agency. She's the head of case management." He nods at my response, not bothering to really acknowledge anything I said. "Anyway, thanks for your help, man. Let me know if you need anything in return."

That goes in one ear and out the other, he doesn't respond. Walking out of the tech-room, I run into Ghost who is smiling from ear to ear.

"Regan woke up in a great fucking mood," he boasts, his eyes shining and his hair disheveled. "Sucked me off like a fucking vacuum." I laugh with him as he walks with me and grabs the file from my arm.

"Take that to Keres for final reporting, I will catch up with you later." With a pat on the back, I start to walk away but he grabs me.

"Listen, before I go you should know, she woke up in tears. I know that she thought you were dead, but she is new to this world. She was completely unprepared for the expectations and what it is like when we come back from the mission. Then none of us bothered to do aftercare with her after our group session. We have to do better with her." My heart sinks in my chest. She thought I was dead?

"What do you mean?" My fingers clench in my fists, if someone fucking told her something...

"When we came back from the mission, apparently she was asking about you and everyone was blowing her off. No one would tell her, then she was scolded about her not helping out and just standing around. The crew assumed we had prepared her and were upset she wasn't jumping in to help." Blowing out a breath of air, I nod and try to figure out how to approach this. He nods before taking off in the other direction. Making my way back to the room, I want to talk to Regan about what exactly she's feeling. That would explain why she was so stressed when she saw me a few days ago.

There was a lot of shit happening, and I was needed in ten places at once. There were debriefings, notes, reports, and of course I had to talk to Shark about what happened when I was face to face with Kastilof. He especially wanted to know how he got away. Top that off with making arrangements for our fallen brother in arms and sending the message to everyone.

"Maverick!" She beams at me as I push through the shared door. Her hair is sticking up several ways, her lips chapped slightly as she lounges lazily. Our perfect little cum dumpster.

"I missed you, baby." Crawling into bed with her feels natural, and when she curls into my side, I swear she starts purring like a kitten. "I actually wanted to talk to you about something."

"Uh oh, I don't like deep talks with Maverick," she groans as she cocoons further into the bed.

Laughing at her, I pull the blankets higher up our bodies. "It's not that bad. I just wanted to talk about what happened on the mission and what led to you believing I was dead.."

"Ugh," she groans again, this time with a pout. "Ghost told you about my emotional breakdown this morning, didn't he?"

"Don't try to be upset with him for telling me. It's our job to take care of you.. Plus, I heard some things and wanted to know what was up."

"I thought you were dead, okay?" She snarls, her entire face glowing bright red with the tears that brim her eyes.

"Woah," I mutter, bringing her curled form closer to me and kissing the top of her head. "Tell me what happened."

"No one would tell me where you were, and there was a dead guy that they wouldn't tell me who that was. I couldn't find you, I panicked, and I was barely calm enough when Ghost distracted me."

"That's a pretty good distraction," I mutter into her hair as I plant a gentle kiss to the crown of her head. "You know that I'm alive, obviously, but I was helping make funeral arrangements for the family of the individual we lost. He was an original member of the club, and it really struck a chord within the club having lost him. He actually taught Ghost how to flay a guy." I didn't really expect a laugh, but her giggle brings me a sliver of joy that I need.

"I didn't know where you were and no one would tell me. I guess I get why they wouldn't know because you were all mourning a member, but I was so scared Maverick." The hurt in her voice ran bone deep for me too, and I couldn't imagine the way she was feeling right now. Fuck, I would rage and burn the world if I thought she died.

"Not seeing you immediately was hell, but it's a routine for me to do this stuff. Being the sergeant-at-arms on top of going into the first mission led by me, I had a lot of responsibilities to take care of when I got back to the club. It is my job to report directly to Shark, who had a lot of questions. I have reports, notes, debriefings, and I had to contact the family of the fallen brother. I came as quickly as I could, but I will be more mindful for the next mission we go on. We should have done better to prepare you for what missions are like and what to expect. I promise that next time you will know exactly what to expect and what your role will be when we return from the mission. I am sorry for not ensuring you were that way this time." She nods into the crevice of my neck, her hot breath fanning me as she snuggles even deeper. I don't know how it's entirely possible, but this girl loves her sleep.

"You shouldn't have to change what you do for me," she says softly, and I know that's her self-doubt talking almost immediately. Forcing her head out of my neck, I make her look at me dead in the eyes.

"If you need extra reassurance, I want you to tell me. You aren't a burden to us. We *chose* you. Our sick, twisted fucking selves found a female who takes it all in stride. You're our Little Pyro that stumbled into our crimson catacomb for the better."

"I love you," she whispers so softly I'm not sure I heard her clearly. She smiles lovingly at me, and it's all the confirmation I need. Bringing my lips down to hers, telling her everything I am so scared to admit and more.

After pulling away, I stare into her hypnotic eyes and realize she's my everything. *Our* everything. "We love you too."

I use my free hand to undo the button on my pants. My cock comes out easily as I shimmy my pants down lower. Regan rolls her leg upward, I grab her soft hip and I slide into her easily. Her warm, wet cunt is like home, and there is no place I would rather be.

Canada: Text HOME to 686868 for Self-Harm Help
USA: Text CONNECT to 741741 for Self-Harm Help
UK: Text SHOUT to 85258 for Self-Harm Help

Made in the USA
Columbia, SC
11 June 2025